A DISCOVERY TO DIE FOR

BONNIE ELIZABETH

My Big Fat Orange Cat Publishing

A Discovery to Die For
My Big Fat Orange Cat
Mystery 2020

My Big Fat Orange Cat Publishing
MyBigFatOrangeCat.com

ISBN 978-0-9980829-9-8 trade paperback
978-1-953363-06-0 large print

Chapter 1

Just when I thought life was sorting itself out, I arrived at my acupuncture clinic to find a body in the parking lot.

I didn't realize it was a body, as in dead body, at first. It was just sitting there up against the metal support that ran between my office and the pizza place next door. I thought from the set of the body and the style of hair that it was a woman. Her head was angled funny, but when you find a body, your first thought isn't that they're dead. Not really. At least mine wasn't.

I'm Ash Jericho and I'm an acupuncturist in Seales, Kentucky. I was getting ready for a short day of treating patients—my practice was still new because I'd been living out of town for years—and had come around from the side where I'd parked my car. Normally the blacktop parking lot that overlooks the highway that runs from Seales to Frankfort catches an assortment of garbage overnight. I wanted to clean up before work.

It's one reason I go through the front, rather than the back. I also hate the stink of the dumpster back there. Fortunately, it's not right by my door or I'd have turned down the office. I'd had enough trepidation about setting up out here. I'd had this dream of a homey place downtown where the red brick buildings were all about three stories tall and narrow. Old houses sat just around the corner and most of them had been converted to commercial businesses. I'd had that sort of homey look back in the Northwest where I'd practiced before returning home. I had thought I'd get it again here, but nothing had opened up.

So, I'd grabbed this, an office in this newer little strip mall in front the big grocery store right on the highway. Visibility, you know.

Which was another reason it was weird to find a body there. People start grocery shopping early in Seales. We are a farm community, after all. Of course, the body was in the front of the office, not the back. There was plenty of traffic running along the highway and the noise of cars and occasional hoots from behind me kept me company as I approached the woman sitting there.

By that time, I was pretty certain she was

dead, though I was still in denial. I mean, yeah, I smelled the faint traces of copper and something that reminded of a dirty diaper, but I wanted to tell myself that she'd just fallen asleep waiting for a pizza fix. Maybe she used drugs or something and was hungry?

Except there was a burgundy stain on the front of her shirt. I stopped walking and swallowed hard. I pinched myself. I stepped closer to her, careful not to mess up anything in the almost too-clean parking lot. I reach out a hand to check the pulse in her neck, hating the cool feel of her skin and the fact that nothing moved in her neck.

I pulled back, feeling gross, wanting to wash my hands, but instead I got out my cell phone and called the police. I used the emergency number, though I had the number of the detective that would probably get the case.

My heart started to beat a bit faster, not just because I was reporting a body but because I anticipated seeing Detective Byron Cabot. He was the main detective on the Seales police force and he got all the "big" cases, so to speak. Rarely murder, though I had met him when my cousin Marty was murdered. She hadn't been the only death at the time, but Byron had been the one person who hadn't decided I was the prime suspect, at least he hadn't acted like it.

I mean, yeah, I suppose the fact that Marty

had challenged our grandmother's will leaving everything to me was motive but, sadly, I hadn't really cared. I was home and had planned to start up my acupuncture business no matter what. Unfortunately, my ex hadn't known that and had set out on something of a killing spree trying to make sure that I stayed in town.

I'd almost ended up a victim. I'd spent half a year getting over that and trying to rebuild a reputation that meant people would trust me with their health, and now here was a body in front of my clinic.

The woman sitting dead in front of the building had picked a pretty spring morning to die. Although if she'd been killed, perhaps she wasn't the one who had picked it? The sky was just pinking up over in the east, clear of any clouds.

I eyed the darkened windows of the other businesses in this little strip mall, while listening to a car that sounded like it needed a new muffler. A pale blue Honda CRV drove up the entry to the shopping area towards the grocery store and pharmacy. Beyond it sat the Burger King.

Around the corner was a McDonald's and a Bojangles. Taco Bell was a few blocks further up on a corner with just a gas station and its building. Seales is set for eating, so long as it's fast food.

I glanced back in my office, which was dark

and I had downed the shades, leaving only a small crack for a bit of light. The tax preparation place looked pretty quiet too, which was a change from earlier, before taxes had been due. To the right was the pizza place which never had blinds drawn. They were always busy once they opened. I had worried about that at first, but I had talked to the chiropractor who had his office on the other side of the pizza place.

He'd suggested soft music was enough to drown out any sounds from the take-out place and it seemed to work just fine. I had a feeling I might move someday, but for now this worked. On the other side of the chiropractor was a pet store and a small salon where you could get your hair and nails done. I'd used them for my hair but did my own nails, though my friend Cheri thought their manicures were to die for.

Which was probably not the best description given the woman in front of me. Now that I was back to looking at her, I was surprised that I didn't recognize her. Seales is a small rural community and while I'd been gone to acupuncture school and then practicing in the Northwest for some time, I had grown up here. I'd been back for months and I'd been re-acquainted with a lot of old friends, yet I didn't recognize this woman's face.

Soon enough, in response to my call, a blue

and white police car turned into the parking lot, coming just a bit too fast, not hitting the brakes quite enough, and the car appeared about to overturn. The driver, however, managed to avoid doing so, for which I was thankful. Nothing like having the police have an accident when you've called in a dead body.

I was also thankful because I had two patients coming in that morning. I didn't want to disturb their treatments because the police had been driving recklessly.

The car parked across three parking spaces right in front of where the dead body lay. I stepped over to the officer as he started to get out of his car.

"Stay back, ma'am," he said. I recognized Officer Gil Daffney. I talked to him back when Marty was killed and later on when her friend, Officer Claire Wilcox, had died. He was young, blond, rather handsome in that too young, almost innocent way. He was also, apparently, just a bit reckless when driving.

I waited while he got out of the car and looked at the body. He spoke into his radio and then stopped, looking at me.

"Ms. Jericho?" he said.

I nodded.

"You found the body?"

Another nod.

"Can you tell me what you were doing here?" Gil took out some paper.

"I was about to open my office," I told him, nodding at the door of the acupuncture office.

"Are you a receptionist or something?"

"I'm an acupuncturist," I explained patiently.

Gil raised his eyebrows as if that was an odd thing. Maybe in Seales or wherever he grew up, it was. It certainly wasn't for me. Daffney might act like he was a Seales native, but I knew for a fact he wasn't. His family was from the western part of Kentucky, not the north-central area. Not that that was a problem or anything.

"Did you close up last night?" he asked.

"I did. About four. I didn't have patients scheduled after that." I suppose if I were good, I'd have sat around until five, hoping for a walk-in. Instead, I'd finished my appointments and the paperwork I needed to do and left.

"And there wasn't a body there then?" Daffney clarified.

"Nope," I said. "I'm sure someone at the pizza place would have noticed it," I said, helpfully reminding him that they were open until midnight, two in the morning on Friday and Saturday.

Daffney nodded and looked at the body.

"Did you know her?" he asked.

"I don't recognize her."

"Really?" he looked at me like I was an idiot.

I shrugged. "Not been back for very long," I said.

"Layla Wiltshire, the herbalist?" Daffney said. "I'd have thought you two would have been great buddies?"

I shook my head, although a knot formed in my stomach. I had had online interactions with Layla and they hadn't been pleasant. She seemed to think that her background of reading up on herbs on google meant that she was as qualified to treat people as my degree made me. That did not go over well with me, particularly when she'd started telling people I was overcharging them for my treatments.

Her picture online was a picture of a cone flower, not a face, so I'd never seen her.

It wasn't going to do my business any good to have her dead on my doorstep.

Chapter 2

Daffney made a call on the radio that squawked on his shoulder like some sort of electronic parrot. I made out a few different voices along with plenty of static, but I couldn't have said whether they were male or female. Byron Cabot arrived a few minutes later.

My heart always beats a little faster when Byron is around. I get a tingle in my belly that has nothing to do with food. He's around average height for a man, which puts him a bit taller than I am. He's dark haired with high cheekbones marking him as having some Native American blood. I'd found out that the tribe his mother was from were Choctaw, but he'd never been on a reservation nor did he pay much attention to his tribal background.

"Ash Jericho," Byron said slowly, giving me a nod. He didn't smile, not really, though there was a twinkle in his dark eyes that gave me a thrill. Damn, the man was nice to look at even if he did move into a relationship with all the speed of molasses in January.

"Detective," I said, trying to maintain a certain level of formality. Did Daffney know we were seeing each other off and on? It wasn't like we were a couple, not really. I mean, unless you counted the few dinners and coffees and the occasional bout of sitting together in the romantic atmosphere of the city planning commission.

It wasn't completely Byron's fault. First, I'd been a suspect and we couldn't see each other. Then he'd been awkward about asking me out, particularly in light of the fact that I'd just survived not only being attacked but attacked by an ex-boyfriend, who he worried that I might have feelings for. Fortunately, I'd been able to set him straight on that particular aspect. Finally, he'd also worried that I might still be in mourning. I can't say he was wrong about that, but it wouldn't have meant turning down a meal with him.

Now and again, we'd made plans, but Byron's job got in the way. It's not like Seales is a hot bed of crime or anything, but when there is a crime, it's not always when it's convenient for those who have to investigate it. Last time, we'd exchanged one kiss that suggested it might not stay the chaste little peck, but he'd gotten a call and had to leave.

Perhaps that's why he was interested in taking it slow. He wanted to be sure I could handle the inconsistency of his job. We hadn't really talked about "our relationship," so it was hard to know. I'd talked to my friend Lisa back in Portland. Neither of us had a clue. Lisa had suggested just jumping his bones, but she wasn't here. I mean, I didn't want the reputation I might get if I did something like that and things didn't work out. Seales is a small town.

It's one reason I'd avoided talking to Cheri too much, although she'd thought this was strangely slow as well.

Cheri's always been good at getting information. She had all her feelers out to try and find out what Byron's problem was. She wasn't sure about him testing me because of his odd work hours. Cheri's ideas tended towards a psychotic wife locked in an attic that he didn't want me to know about. Not that any of her feelers had suggested there was any truth to the matter, but the facts didn't keep Cheri from bringing that up. She might have been a Bronte in a past life.

Byron knelt down, looking at the body. He didn't touch anything. Another car drove up. Another officer with a camera got out and he came over to talk to Byron. The new officer, who I didn't recognize, started taking pictures. This was going to be a long morning.

"Can I go in my office?" I asked. "I have patients who are due here soon."

"Can you change the appointments?" Byron asked. "It'd be better if there were fewer people in the parking lot. This area's a crime scene, though you can go to your office. If they insist on coming, have them go through the back door and park over in the grocery store lot."

I nodded and headed to my door.

"Can you go around the back and open that door? In case there's something on the front door or window?" Byron asked, watching me as I got close to the glass door.

I smiled at him, though it was likely a little tight. I walked around the building, which was cream brick with dark wood beams here and there. I wasn't sure if the beams did anything in particular or if they were just for show. The side area had no concrete walk, just blacktop, so I walked on the parking lot side. The dumpster was on the other side, thank heavens, and I didn't have to pass that.

While the front of the building had large windows, the back had no such thing. I'd have to prop my door open so that people would know to come through there. The back lot was wider and set up so that large trucks could easily park and make deliveries. There were no real spaces for people.

The sounds of people at the grocery store were louder back there, and I smelled cigarette smoke, probably from the employees of the pizza place. I knew they took smoke breaks by their backdoor, though I wished they wouldn't. I wasn't their boss, and without laws keeping folks from smoking by doors, there wasn't a lot I could do. The laws against smoking near doorways in the Northwest had spoiled me.

I opened the back and headed towards the reception area where I had my computer and the printed appointment schedule. I print out a schedule daily, just in case, though I try to use the computer when I put in names.

My office is long and narrow. There's a large waiting area on the right side in the front. On the left is a smallish reception area with a large desk blocking people from walking back into that area. There's a door to a hallway, which bisects the building all the way to the back door.

I have two rooms on either side. The one closest to the reception area keeps herbal formulas and patient records behind lock and key. The other three are for use. The massage therapist uses the one in the back just in front of the room that is basically a small kitchen where we can eat lunch or take a break. There's a small bathroom on the other side.

I use the two rooms across the hall from the reception area, behind the waiting area. Mostly I used the back one, but if I ever got busy enough, I'd use the front one, too. It wouldn't be quite as pleasant hearing people talking up front, but I didn't have a lot of choice.

I called Mrs. Platt, my first patient, to let her know that there had been a problem in the parking area. I explained that she'd have to park in the grocery store lot and come in through the back. I told her I'd have the door open for her.

Mrs. Platt seemed pleased enough, but she's easily pleased. She goes to the same church my parents go to, and I've known her forever. She has arthritis in her hands, which keeps her from crocheting as much as she'd like. It also causes some problems gardening.

Then I called Ryan Dushane. Ryan works across the way at the grocery store. He does a lot of stocking and has developed back problems. He's been hoping acupuncture would help, and so far it has. He only comes in once a month now, usually on his lunch hour, which is when his appointment was.

I'd done what I could, but I wasn't changing appointments. Thursdays tended to be slow and I needed every patient I could get if I was to keep running a business. This was particularly true if people were going to die in the parking lot.

I breathed in, reminding myself that no matter how this affected me, a woman had died. A woman that I might not have liked very much, but a human being. My needs weren't the most important here. It helped a little, though not as much as I liked. Images of Marty, not that I'd found Marty, kept coming up. The only way I was going to get through this was through practical worries and not being overly empathetic.

I went through my morning procedures while I listened for Mrs. Platt. I went into the back room of my two rooms and made sure the sheets were all smooth and comfortable on my table. I checked to be sure nothing else was out of place. I cleaned up the kitchen area a bit more than normal because I'd have people walking by it.

While patients went back there to find the bathroom, most people didn't notice the kitchen when I had a large sign for the bathroom. I didn't want people accidentally going out the back door and then be unable to come inside.

I texted Pam Galloway, the massage therapist, to let her know what was going on. We didn't normally see each other on Thursdays, but if she happened to show up or have an unexpected patient, I didn't want her to be surprised.

Pam sent me a shocked face and asked if they'd be done by the next day.

I said I didn't know but that I hoped so. I had a feeling the pizza place was really going to be upset if the police were still there later on. How long could it take? I almost hit myself for thinking that. I'd been involved in police investigations at least once before and they took as long as they took, usually much longer than anyone wanted them to go on.

"Oh, my!" Mrs. Platt said, entering through the back door. She was hobbling a bit in her white running shoes. She always came in gray sweat pants and a t-shirt, sometimes with a sweat jacket over the top if it was cold. Her graying hair was trimmed short, and she had slightly narrow eyes and almost pointed ears that gave her an elfin look.

"Did you get a decent spot?" I asked.

She waved a hand, the index finger swollen with her arthritis but not red. A slight improvement but not as good as the week before.

"Whoever parks out there?" she asked me.

I nodded and led her into the treatment room. She was used to the routine and although she's slow to undress and arrange her clothing, we've got a system worked out. I went out to the front while she changed and watched the police from my window.

I noticed they had sawhorses set up around the perimeter and a car had just been turned away. Someone else trying to get to work.

I hoped that things would be quieter by the time I finished with Mrs. Platt. Byron came in while she was on the table, the needles in, working to make the changes her body needed. I was filling an herbal formula to help her, too.

"Do you have time for questions?" he asked.

"I have a patient on the table, but then I have two hours after that," I said.

Byron nodded. He looked at the clock. "How long until she's done?"

"About twenty minutes or so," I said.

He was dressed in dark trousers of a heavy material that wore well. They never seemed to look wrinkled on him, and I often wondered if he was fantastic with an iron—something that would definitely be a talent I'd put to use—or if the material was just that kind of material. He had on a long-sleeved blue button-down shirt. It was a nice look on him, the blue highlighting the darkness of his hair.

He went back out and started talking to officers while I finished the formula and made some notes on Mrs. Platt's chart. I went back to take needles out. We spent a few minutes chatting at the front while she made her next appointment, and then I walked with her towards the back of the building.

I hadn't even made it down the hallway when I heard the bell of the front door. Byron was standing there with Officer Daffney, both of whom looked altogether too serious.

Chapter 3

My hands started to sweat as I walked down the hall. I wondered what was wrong. Byron looked as if he weren't pleased. I heard a car door slam through the open back door, and I nearly jumped.

"Have a seat," Byron said, gesturing to the chairs in my waiting room. I have a blue love seat and two club chairs. I grabbed my favorite blue and green striped club chair and sat down. An espresso wood coffee table sat in the middle of the seating arrangement. Byron took the love seat leaving the other club chair for Daffney.

"You said you didn't know who the woman outside was, is that correct?" Daffney asked.

I nodded.

"But you had interacted with her on social media?" Daffney pressed.

"As I said, I hadn't ever met her in person. Her image on social media is that of a cone flower."

"But she has photos of herself on her profile if you look at them," Daffney said.

I shrugged. "I didn't know her. We only interacted a couple of times in groups where she would try and tell people that she knew more about herbal medicine than I did," I said. I did not add that I had the education and she didn't. That wasn't the point.

"Still, you interacted and you didn't go look at her profile to find out more about her?" Daffney pressed.

"I guess I wasn't curious enough," I said. I wanted to snap. I was keeping myself under control just barely.

"This isn't the first murder that you've been questioned in," Daffney said.

I glanced at Byron. He was being quiet, but I saw a slight redness creep up from his collar.

"What is this?" I asked. "As you have a confession from someone else in those murders, I'm not sure how that relates."

"It was your ex-boyfriend," Daffney said. "It's certainly possible that he was covering for you."

"Really?" I looked at Byron about ready to scream at him.

His face was beet red now, the sort that makes you worry that someone is going to have a stroke or something.

"I can't be in charge of this investigation," Byron said, "as we know each other." What he wasn't saying was that we'd dated and now he couldn't be the officer in charge. "That could also make anything done in the previous investigation put into question."

"So, do I need an attorney because I found a body outside my business?" I snapped at Daffney.

"There's no need to get hostile," Daffney said mildly, writing something down.

"I found a body outside my place of business, a business that I love, by the way. I called 911 as soon as I realized there was a problem. I didn't recognize the woman because the only interaction we have had was on social media and she was the one who instigated those interactions. I have done nothing wrong. If you need a further statement about any past incidents, I'll need an attorney present."

"If there's nothing to hide, why do you need an attorney?" Daffney asked.

"Because you seem to think I did this," I said.

"It seems that the last officer who thought you

murdered someone ended up dead," Daffney pointed out.

This was true enough, though I hadn't killed her.

I glared at him. "If this is the way the questioning is going to go, I'd like to call my attorney. We can set up an appointment to meet at the station later on. However, I have an appointment in just over an hour and I'd like to be able to do my job."

Daffney sighed, glancing at Byron. Byron's face was still red and looked like stone. I wondered what he wasn't saying.

"I'd like to know more about what you noticed when you got to work," Daffney added.

I went through what I had noticed about the body. I told him where I parked. He wanted to know why I didn't go in through the back. I explained that I didn't like the loading dock and the dumpster right there. I talked about the trash that was often left around the parking lot and how I picked up what was left outside of my office before coming in for the day.

"Did you pick up anything this morning?" Daffney asked.

I shook my head.

"It was pretty clean this morning," he observed.

I nodded, thinking that it had been unusually

clean. A murderer who cleaned up? Or had Layla Wiltshire been cleaning up the area when she'd been killed.

Daffney played with the pen he was holding as he thought about what to ask next. The click click of the pen sliding up and down through its tiny mechanism was beginning to annoy me.

Daffney asked a few more questions, always with the pen sounds, and then he set the pen down and put the notebook in his pocket and looked at Byron.

Byron still looked livid. I didn't envy Daffney when they got outside. As a detective, Byron's authority was greater than Daffney's even if he wasn't on the case. I had a feeling he was going to use it.

I nodded at them as they left.

When they were gone, it was too silent in the office. Usually the pizza place is open and they're walking around making pizza dough. I normally had music on in thc waiting area, but hadn't bothered because no one would be waiting there. It was just me, the faint sounds of the police outside, who didn't talk much as they worked, and the faint smells of herbs. Thank heavens I hadn't been using a lot of moxa in the last few days. That always smells vaguely like marijuana. I suspected Officer Daffney wouldn't have believed my protests that it was a legal herb rather than one that wasn't legal in Kentucky.

I sighed, noticing the pen.

I reached for it, hesitating. One of the reasons I'd inherited my grandmother's fortune was because, like her, I'm psychic. I'm not like all-knowing telepathic or anything, but when I touch things, I get impressions. She'd spent much of my childhood teaching me to control what images I let in.

The other thing I can do is see the ghost of her favorite cat, Penelope Blue. Sometimes I think I was left the inheritance to keep the cat company. With Gram, it had probably been a consideration.

I normally didn't go around grabbing items just to get a sense of the person who had held them. It felt like cheating or like peeping into places that someone else might not want me to know about.

It was a testament to how angry and upset I was with Officer Daffney that I only argued with myself about the ethics of picking up the pen for fifteen seconds.

It was a cheap pen with a bank name on it. The plastic cover was still warm from Daffney's hand. I felt irritation and fatigue. My eyes wanted to close, though I knew I was awake. Annoyance hit. Another call. I sensed Daffney's hatred of the work shift he was on.

Red hot anger ran through me, making me want to run outside screaming in rage, though I knew it wasn't mine but left over from Daffney. I wanted to break things, throw things. Oddly the object of my rage was Byron. Byron had been angry because Daffney, if he was the pen holder, had done something wrong. There was a sense of embarrassment too, as if Daffney knew Byron was right but didn't want to admit it. I also got a thrill of hope that he could take down Byron, to get even for whatever it was that Byron had done.

That was all. While Daffney had had the pen for some time, he clearly wasn't that bonded to it. The emotions were strong, but they weren't overwhelming. I always knew who I was, which meant this wasn't the best thing to pick up to try and understand Daffney. Not that I wanted to understand him. I wondered, though, how much of his hard grilling was about his anger with Byron and not because he really thought I'd killed Layla.

Still, not good to be a murder suspect. I glanced at the time. I had some time before Ryan came in. I went to the break room where I kept my purse in a drawer. I took out my cell phone and called Cheri. I wanted to get the scoop on Daffney. If anyone would know, it'd be Cheri.

Unfortunately, her phone rang and rang. It was early, and Cheri worked as a barista. Chances were she was still serving. I hung up without leaving a message. If it was important, I'd have texted her because she'd see that before she'd listen to a message. Even so, I knew that my number would show up and Cheri would call me when she could.

I considered calling my aunt. Aunt Daisy and I had become close since she'd moved into the big house that had belonged to Gram. It was my idea. Daisy was now renting out her little place and it gave her a nice income. She liked being a bit financially independent.

After Rick Darlington had tried to kill me and broken a window in the carriage house out back, my home had become a crime scene. Then the window had to be fixed before I could move back out. It took long enough that I had gotten somewhat comfortable in the big house.

Although I intended to move out and have my space again, I kept putting it off. Gram's house was large enough that I felt like I had space, but there were still people around. I liked that. I felt safer there, though I hated that I did so.

Being in the same house with Daisy had given us a closeness we hadn't had before, and I liked being able to chat with her. I'd even confessed to having Gram's gift of touching something and knowing things. Daisy had accepted that news in a way my mother never had. She agreed it wasn't something she'd discuss with my mother, either.

For that I was grateful. Still, her support went a long way in making me feel normal.

I wasn't at all surprised that my desire to talk to someone led me to think of Daisy before I thought of my own mother. In fact, it had been almost a week since I'd spoken to either of my folks. I made a mental note to check in with my dad. He and I got along far better than my mother and I.

I was at loose ends and not sure what to do. The officer investigating the murder clearly had issues with Byron, which didn't sit well with me, particularly since the woman murdered had already tried to bad mouth my business. I had to wonder what was so wrong with me wanting to be back with family in Kentucky. I had lived just outside of Portland, a real city, a place where there was actual crime, for almost fifteen years and I had never once been accused of a crime. In less than a year, I was being accused twice.

I went up to the front desk to try and do some work. There were always outstanding bills and collections to look over. Seating myself in the comfortable black computer chair that I had purchased for the front desk, I picked up one of the pens from the silver mesh pencil holder I had.

I wasn't paying attention and let images rush into me, images that weren't mine.

I heard a voice that said, "I'll make her pay

one way or another!" Fear arched through me, and then the image was gone.

I put the pen down, looking at it. It was from the chiropractor a few doors down. The voice I'd heard wasn't his. The voice couldn't have been talking about him, either. Whoever had to pay was a her.

I felt chills run down my spine as I stared at the little blue pen, wondering if the her in the vision I had had was Layla or if it was me.

Chapter 4

It took me quite some time to get myself back together. Ryan was walking in the back door as I was finishing a final meditation to try and stop my hands from shaking. That was not the sort of thing anyone wants in their acupuncturist!

Fortunately, I was calm enough to make chart notes and then treat him. Ryan is just a little older than I am. He had worked as at the grocery store since it had opened about three years ago. Cheri had told me about the opening, how our contractors had worked hard to try and get the store done before the target date.

After I got Ryan on the table and inserted the needles without shaking hands, I went back to the front to try and calm myself. Half of my reaction had to be leftover stress from Marty's death. I would normally have been empathetic towards Layla's family and friends, and here I was worried about me and my business. It was all I could think about, as if caring for this woman or her family would completely undo whatever peace I had come to after they had arrested Rick Darlington for the murder of my cousin and her friend.

I worked on calming my breath and focusing on my business while Ryan rested on the table, or, as we say in acupuncture land, "cooked." I even stood and did a bit of tai chi, which I found calming, though there wasn't enough room to do the full form. When he was done, I went in to pull needles, finally beginning to feel like myself.

As we were checking out at the front desk, he asked about what was going on. Working across the way, he couldn't help but see.

"I believe it was Layla Wiltshire, at least that's what I'm told," I said.

"Odd woman," Ryan said. He was checking his phone to see when he could make an appointment for a month from now.

"I only interacted with her online," I said. "She wasn't always pleasant."

Ryan smiled. "That was Layla. She tended to be kind of difficult. She thought we needed to have more organic fresh herbs, and she was just the one to sell them to us. The problem is, we have to inspect how someone grows things. There are licenses that need to be in place for us to purchase from someone, but she wasn't interested in that. She just thought we should accept her offering from her small business. She got really mad at the store manager and threatened to boycott us. No one really paid attention because it's a drive to go anywhere else. Now and then she'd come in, but she'd glare at anyone she saw. Nancy, who runs the self-service check-out, would always hide when she came through."

"Layla sounds like she was very unhappy," I said. It was a wishy washy response, but there was a fine line between gossiping about people with a patient and listening. I really wanted to listen because who knew what gossip might give me information?

"Probably," Ryan agreed, "and she wanted everyone around her to be equally unhappy."

"Some people are just like that. It's too bad. I think that her herbal knowledge could have been a grcat complcment to mine. I could have referred people to her. In fact, I think she found out about me when I did refer someone. It's kind of ironic that she kept saying I didn't know what I was doing and people should go to her first."

"She did know herbs, particularly those that could be grown in the area." Ryan paused, thinking. "I'm not sure I'd have trusted her with my health, though, you know?"

"I didn't meet her, so I'm not sure I do. Still, I think for me, I understand what my education gave me, so I'd prefer someone who had some formal learning."

Ryan agreed and we finished making his next appointment before he left through the back door.

I watched him go. He'd still been frowning as if there was something else he wanted to say but wasn't quite sure how to say it. I was about to peek out the front and let the police know I was done for the day. They could reach me on my cell phone if they needed me.

As if my thought made it happen, the very same cell phone began to ring. I hurried back up front to answer, thankful for the reprieve from talking to the police again. I had no desire to interact with Officer Daffney again just yet.

Normally, I'd have stayed through the afternoon in case someone showed up. I liked being able to answer questions, and I got about one person a week just walking in to talk to me while checking the place out. Early on it had been more, but I think those who had to see to believe had all been in. While I might have worried about closing early, it wasn't like anyone was going to come in with the police out front. Even if they did, chances were the officers would direct them around back.

I wondered how the pizza place was going to

fare. Small businesses can't take the hit of being involuntarily closed for too long.

Looking at my phone screen, I saw Cheri's name.

"So? What's up this morning? I heard that there were police over by your office," Cheri said without much of a greeting.

"I found a woman dead outside my office—well, the pizza place next door—when I came in this morning," I said.

"Not Layla Wiltshire?! I heard she'd died and maybe it was murder or something, but I didn't even quite put the two together, although maybe I did a little bit," Cheri said. Cheri tends towards a breathless way of speaking. When she gets excited, she can be really over the top. This was clearly one of those times.

"That was her," I said. "And naturally, because she bad mouthed me, the cops are now looking at me."

"Oh, Byron wouldn't think it was you!" Cheri said. "Even if he's taking things abnormally slow, he couldn't think you were a killer."

"I guess our relationship means he can't investigate the murder. For now, the officer on the scene, Officer Daffney, is the one investigating. He seems to have no problem believing I could murder someone. In fact, he intimated that pinning Marty's murder on my obsessed ex would be quite convenient. After all, Rick was obsessed, so he'd do anything for me, right?" I have to admit that line of questioning had really pissed me off.

"Oh, that's just sick. Where are we getting these officers lately? I should write the mayor, or better still have my mother do it. In fact, she may be able to take him out to lunch and give him a piece of her mind—well, my mind, you know?"

"Of course, that begs the question of who would want to murder Layla," I said.

Cheri paused. "Well, there's plenty of gossip about her saying the wrong thing to the wrong person. You aren't the only one she's bad-mouthed. There's the chiropractor, not the one in your building, at least not that I've heard, but the one downtown, and there's the health food store downtown that she's bashed. I think she even got into with Justine at the bookstore, and you know that Justine would know all about murder. Not that I think she'd do it."

Justine ran a mystery bookstore, new and used, and it was quite the thing downtown. She got local authors, and sometimes not so local authors, to come in and do readings and signings at least once a month. She sold a lot of books online as well, which I'd heard was what kept the store afloat.

"I've heard that Danielle at the Hoskins stables hated her too," Cheri said. "Something about saying they weren't taking good care of their horses."

"In other words, Layla wasn't popular," I said.

"Nope. Which I hate to say is going to make finding out who did kill her all that much harder. I can only think that they put her by your door to make people think you did it. Which means someone doesn't like you. Or else Layla was there for some other reason and they killed her. Has the pizza place had a health inspection recently?"

I tried to file away all the names of people that didn't like Layla, but it was hard to keep track. I hoped that I'd be able to come with another suspect for the police so they'd stop looking at me. This was all I needed while trying to build up my business. The way things were going, I could fail before I even got started.

Chapter 5

I got home mid-afternoon. The sun was high in the sky, which was clear and blue. It wasn't going to stay clear, though. I knew storms were forecast for the end of the week, so if I wanted to be outside, today was the day to do it. That's the way it is in May. More rain than sun, though the temperature stayed comfortable.

The trees were fully green, the pink dogwood in the front of the house was just starting to drop its flowers. The gardeners had clearly been there because the whole place smelled like fresh grass. It would be a good afternoon to go for a walk and forget about what was going on. I even considered taking out Blackjax if Daisy hadn't already done so.

Leaving the garage, I walked past the carriage

house, which looked lonely without me in it. The side window had been repaired after Rick had broken through it, but I didn't quite feel safe there. I spent a moment staring at the little place, just two bedrooms and a bath, admiring how nice the white siding looked against the bright blue trim around the windows.

The big house is mostly red brick and white trim. It was home to me, though it wasn't cute the way the carriage house was. I continued towards the side door, my feet scuffing the cement drive as I did so. I hated the fact that the main reason I was still at the big house was because Rick had ruined the safety I felt in the carriage house. I needed to let this go. Perhaps one of the people at the alternative clinic I knew about in Frankfort could be helpful. I made a mental note to give them a call.

I stepped up onto the stoop and opened the door, wondering where Morgan was. Normally he greets me even before I get to the door. I continued into the mud room. It was only then that I heard Morgan's soft steps hurrying through the kitchen to greet me. Win was probably cleaning upstairs. Morgan was getting on in years, so whenever he could avoid cleaning upstairs, he did so. Not that he shirked his duties, but his body was rebelling against the stairs.

I'd done some acupuncture on his knees and

low back, but he wanted to pay me. I didn't want him to. Rather than argue, he had begun to make excuses to avoid treatment. I'd given him the name of the clinic I knew in Frankfort, hoping he'd keep up treatments there.

"I didn't expect you so soon," Morgan said as he greeted me. He's not much taller than I am, and his dark skin is spotted with age spots here and there. His black hair, which he keeps trimmed short, is turning to gray. For all that he talks about getting old, his eyes are still bright and he stands straighter than a lot of my patients. He was dressed in gray trousers and a short-sleeved white shirt striped with blue pinstripes. Over that he wore a light gray vest.

"I didn't expect to be here so soon," I said. "There's a problem at the office."

I headed into the kitchen. It's a huge thing that Gram had redone about ten years ago. It was in Tuscan colors, all lovely rusts, browns and a sort of salmon color that blended well. There were bronze accents in the hardware. The huge island looked out at the gathering room with the large fireplace in brown stone. In the far corner of the kitchen, beyond the cabinets, sat a round table in an eating area. A formal dining room was in the front, just beyond the mud room, but we rarely used it. Like many formal areas, it could easily be closed off when it wasn't in use, which was most of the time.

Even when Gram had been alive, we'd only ever used the formal dining room on holidays. Mostly we ate around the small table and at the island, picking at finger foods, wandering around the house, talking with whoever we wanted. There would be games in the big room in the new wing, which ran behind the great room. That, too, remained somewhat closed off from the rest of the house.

"What's going on?" Daisy was at the table in the kitchen. She had a glass of sweet tea in front of her and an empty plate. She'd clearly had a late lunch or perhaps an afternoon snack. The pie that sat on the counter giving off the delicious smell of berries was missing a piece. I suspected the latter.

"I found a dead body in front of the office," I said, slipping into the chair.

"Oh, my word!" Daisy placed a hand to her heart and leaned back. "You cannot be serious!"

I nodded.

She shook her head. Then she reached a hand over to me and patted the back of mine. "How horrible for you."

"It gets worse," I said. "It was Layla Wiltshire. She's bad mouthed me and my clinic on social media. She was actually in front of the pizza place, so that's something, but the fact that it was so close to my office makes me a suspect, *again*."

Daisy took a deep breath and shook her head. You'd think she'd be one of the people who was most angry with me when I'd been accused of her daughter's murder, but she was one of my staunchest supporters.

"This is just horrible, particularly because your business appears to be targeted," Daisy said.

It was an interesting point and not one I'd thought about earlier. What if it was my business and not me personally? Cheri's last idea about the pizza place made sense too. What if one of our businesses was being targeted?

If Layla had problems with the Hoskins farm for potentially mistreating their horses, what about the pet store? I didn't think they sold animals, but I hadn't visited it. I had only glanced inside through their big front window.

"Does the Sassy Pet sell pets or just food?" I asked.

Morgan was making me a sandwich, not that he'd asked me about food nor had I asked him, but he did things like that. Sometimes I wonder if he was comfortable with Gram's psychic abilities because he had some of his own.

My stomach growled as I watched him work while talking to Daisy.

"Just food," Daisy said. "I go there sometimes to get things for Hellspark and Babs."

Hellspark and Babs are Gram's last Siamese cats. Both were regal chocolate point Siamese, her favorite breed. As if she didn't want me to forget her, Penelope Blue leaped on the chair next to mine and poked her ghostly little head up over the table. She looks real to me, but Aunt Daisy doesn't see her. Generally she only pops up now and then, usually when I need to pay attention to something. I wondered what it was here that I needed to pay attention to.

I had once seen my grandmother's ghost, too. She was surprisingly unhelpful, but I guess that's the way it is. You need to work out your own problems when you have them and not expect too much of the dead.

Morgan nodded at Daisy's comment. "We order a lot online, but I've been over there, too, for special treats, particularly shortly after Miz Beauvoir passed. I can't imagine someone taking a dislike to that store. They seem quite careful about what they carry. There is a shop cat that lives in the store, but it isn't up for adoption or anything. They don't keep any cats from a local shelter, but on the weekends they do allow the shelter to have animal adoption days where they have cats in the store or dogs in front of the store. Apparently their shop cat doesn't take kindly to dogs."

I nodded. I'd seen the adoption days on Saturdays because I worked a half day Saturday. I didn't particularly like it as I'd found in the Portland area that people who had to have the weekends could be quite demanding. Once I hit my target of twenty-five patients a week on a regular basis, I'd be changing what days I worked.

"I love their shop cat. She's a beautiful calico and so friendly," Daisy said. She looked around for Gram's cats, or should I say our cats as they were ours now. They both seemed to prefer Daisy to me, at least as far as sleeping, but they were nice enough when I was around. Hellspark even sat on me sometimes, though that was when Babs was on Daisy.

Not that Hellspark was really a lap cat. He'd always been so active. A hellion, Gram had said. Once she'd called him Regis but his habit of running crazily around the house had gotten him renamed Hellspark after a book Gram was reading at the time. Sometimes he got called Parkour largely because he seemed to have his own feline gymnasium around the house. He was quieter now, but still active for a cat of his age.

When I had planned to live in the carriage house, I had thought about getting a cat of my own. While I was in the big house, I had Gram's cats to care for. They were ten, so they weren't young cats any longer, and they'd just suffered a loss. I couldn't imagine inflicting a strange cat on them.

I couldn't see Layla having a problem with the pet store. More likely, if she was worried about the welfare of the animals adopted there, she'd have been upset with the shelter, not at the store. It was possible that she was angry about something the store had sold. Perhaps that bore further investigation.

Ticking off the other businesses in my head, I couldn't think of a reason to be angry about the tax office. It was past the end of tax season and the tax preparation team wasn't open such long hours any longer. Piers Leeson came in ten to five every day, and now and then I saw one of the assistants, but it wasn't the full crew that had been working February to April. If someone had done Layla's taxes improperly, it wouldn't be Layla who had died, so I couldn't see a motive for their office to harm her.

Not that I could see a real motive for anyone, but at least if she was sneaking around the pet store, the pizza place, or beauty salon trying to find dirt—perhaps literally—I could see someone getting angry and perhaps murdering her in a rage-filled moment. But as for the tax preparers, not so much.

Morgan put the sandwich in front of me. Chicken salad today, with plenty of onions and celery and chicken. He'd added some lettuce and put it all on sourdough bread. It was lovely. He brought me a glass of lemonade. He knows I'm not that fond of sweet tea, something he says is barbaric, as well as something I had probably learned while I was living on the west coast.

Honestly, I don't hate sweet tea. I'm just more fond of Win's lemonade, which she always made fresh for Gram and now for me. There's something unbeatable about lemons fresh from the greenhouse, which sat on the property out of sight of the big house. Win uses real sugar and puts in what I believe is just the right amount. It keeps for the day, and it's as good in the evening as it is first thing in the morning.

"I didn't know Layla or anything about her," Daisy said. "I guess we don't move in the same circles."

"I'm under the impression that most people who did know her didn't like her much," I said after swallowing a bite of my sandwich. "I called Cheri and when she called me back on her break, she had some tales. Even one of my patients had a few tales."

"That's too bad. She was probably a very unhappy person."

I grinned, thinking that was the same thing I

had said about her earlier. Maybe Daisy's turn of phrase was rubbing off on me or something.

"Hopefully they won't be trying to pin this on Win or on you," Morgan said. Win had briefly been taken to the police station for Marty's murder. They'd suspected her because Rick had beaten her mother near to death and Win was the last person to see her. He'd also planted a syringe like the one used to murder my cousin in her closet where the police would find it.

The doorbell rang. That was unusual. Normally people, even delivery people, come to the side door. Everyone knows that we only use the formal front when there's something going on, and even then, half the folks come through the side.

Morgan hurried to answer. I heard the low murmur of voices as I ate the sandwich, savoring the flavors of the chicken salad. Morgan and Win were definitely spoiling me. It would be hard to go back to the carriage house and live on my own, even if I only had to run across the driveway to the big house.

Morgan returned and nodded at me. "There's an Elle Mabry here to see you."

I frowned. The name wasn't familiar.

I got up and followed him through the great room and past the large staircase that was perpendicular to the front door. The formal rooms were in front—the dining room, living room, and Gram's study, which had become Morgan's study, though he tried to say it was mine. Hellspark and Babs were on the window seat in there looking up, annoyed at the commotion.

Morgan had put Elle in the living room, which was too much cream and yellow for me. Elle was standing by the front window that looked out over the long driveway to the house. Trees dotted our grassy lawn, which reached quite a distance to the stone fencing that lined the front of the property. The dogwood sat in perfect view.

"Can I help you?" I asked.

Elle was older than I had expected. Her hair was slate gray and her face was lined. Her hands were even more so, from age and not just being out in the sun. Her chin was wattled, and there was enough flesh there to make me think that she'd once been heavier than her thin frame suggested.

"I knew your grandmother slightly," Elle said. "She helped me once, and I was hoping you had her talent."

Elle looked at me expectantly. Morgan backed out of the room to let me talk to her.

No one had ever approached me about using my talent. I had no idea anyone had ever asked Gram, though I knew she helped people now and then. I'd never really used my talent or let it be known, so for a moment I didn't know what to say.

Should I tell this stranger that yes, I did have Gram's talent when I couldn't even tell my best friend or did I send her away, wondering if I could have made her life a bit better?

Chapter 6

It was not what I needed right then. I had enough on my plate. Had someone come to my office needing acupuncture, I would have gladly helped because that's who I am and what I do. But this…this was not a normal thing.

"I'm not sure what you mean," I hedged. I rested my right foot on my left ankle and waited, swaying only slightly as I tried to keep my balance. I knew I was biting my lip, and I hoped my fidgeting wasn't a tell.

Elle looked down, then away. She continued to stand by the window, though her back was to the glass as she faced me. The yellows in the room were a stark contrast to the seriousness of her face. I heard Morgan moving around in the other room and the soft murmur of voices. I wished I could take a time out and run to one of them and ask for assistance in responding to Elle's question.

"Your grandmother touched my mom's necklace and told me where my mom had gone. My mom had dementia and she'd been missing for almost two days. The weather was turning cold that year and I was beside myself."

The tears in Elle's eyes and the simple way she told the story made me think that she was telling the truth.

"I knew Beverly Beauvoir could do things like that. I didn't know she just helped people she didn't know. But I came anyway, taking the chance. It was for my mom."

This was something new. I wondered if Gram had left me the house not only so I could be a companion for Penelope Blue, but so that I would be there to help other folks.

Elle smiled. "I think she only did it for friends and friends of friends. I knew her slightly through Marcus, the man who used to run the stables back when your grandfather was still breeding horses."

I nodded. I barely remembered Marcus. As my grandfather got older, he hadn't as much time to attend to the breeding lines, or maybe he'd lost interest. Gram always said his interest waned, but I wondered if it was age or passion for horses that had worn on him. At any rate, the breeding had been cut back with an eye to curtailing it completely, and Marcus had left to work for another one of the big farms, one that was building up their production.

"I'm not sure I have the same talent as Gram," I said. That was true enough. Gram had said every talent was different, particularly when it came to psychic talent. I had seen her ghost, but she had always believed that you couldn't interact with human ghosts. Clearly I could.

"I have a pen that my son used all the time. Evan's been missing for a month. An adult, the police think he ran out on his husband, but I know better. So does Andy." Elle's lip trembled a bit.

I sighed. I didn't know if I could help, but what if I could see or learn something that would help the police find this woman's son and the man who was apparently Andy's husband.

"Let's settle in the other room," I said finally, leading her to Gram's study.

Hellspark glared at me for inviting this stranger into his realm. Babs had already left. There was a wingback chair in the same greens and creams as the pillows on Hellspark's window seat, and I gestured to that. I took Gram's office chair which was a comfortable chair in cream, though it sat just a little low for me no matter how often I adjusted the height. It was as if it were set for Gram and it was going to let no one else use it.

With the desk at my side instead of in front of me, I was almost touching Elle's knees.

"I don't know if I can help," I said. "And if I do help, please don't use my name, okay? I want to build my acupuncture business, not become someone who has a psychic gift everyone wants to test."

Elle nodded. "I understand. Mrs. Beauvoir didn't like folks talking either, but I have to tell you, most everyone did anyway."

I smiled. I could imagine that. Gram was well known, and such a gift would have been something people talked about. Even I had heard vague things though I never engaged, so intent upon keeping my own talents secret thanks to my mom.

Elle held out the pen. It was a fancy sort of thing. The area I'd hold if I were using it to write was a smooth dark wood, almost mahogany colored. The cap was gold and there was a horse shape upon the top. A gold band circled the middle, and the bottom end, where the ink came out, was also framed in gold.

I opened myself as I held it.

I saw a man giving it as a gift, the pen surrounded by a white box sitting on light foam. The receiver was a man younger than I am now. I had a hunch the face belonged to Andy, but several years ago. I saw the pen being used, the caress always loving. The hand of a person who loved the pen used it to write thank-you notes and quick grocery lists. They also used it to pen letters that they sent off to a friend very far away. I wasn't sure where, only that the friend was incredibly special, and they didn't live close by.

Joy leaped from the pen, and I knew I was smiling as I looked through the memories, mostly vague feelings and images of letters. It was like flipping through a diary. Then there was sadness. The pen was put away more often, used more for signing checks to pay bills. I sensed resentment around the bills, as if the person paying them didn't think they were necessary.

Frustration built. Anger. Another man was there and they were arguing about money. This wasn't the same man who had given the pen. I wondered if this was Andy, though that made me wonder who I had seen offering the pen as a gift. I felt the anger of not just one argument but many. Fear started to grow in my belly, though I didn't understand exactly why.

Then there was nothing else, not exactly. There were other images, memories, but they weren't imprinted with the same level of emotion as the ones I had just seen.

I came back to see Elle watching me, leaning forward, concerned.

"How long?" I asked. Time doesn't mean anything when I'm touching something. Gram had always tried to warn me to watch how deep I went. She'd been my monitor. Normally, I guard myself against images, allowing only a few in at a time. There's not usually a reason for me to want to dig as deep into the memories and impressions as I had wanted to do with the pen.

"Probably ten minutes. Much longer than Mrs. Beauvoir went under," Elle said.

"I didn't see anything that seemed helpful," I said. "I only know what the pen knows. Evan didn't talk about going away when he was holding it. Who gave him the pen?"

"That was Jim Rensler," Elle said. "He was a good friend to my Evan. He didn't shun him when Evan came out, though Jim wasn't gay himself. He gave him the pen when he left to go to college in England. Jim loved it there. He never came back to Kentucky, though he wrote to Evan until a few years ago. Jim died of cancer. Evan was quite broken up—well, we all were. Jim was so young."

I nodded.

"Did Evan have money problems?" I asked, wondering if I could ask if Andy had contributed to them.

Elle shook her head. "I can't imagine he did. He was in IT and made a good living. I'd have helped if he needed more, but how much more can one man, even a man in a relationship, need?

I know Andy didn't make much as a sous chef, but they weren't hurting for money. I don't think."

I hated this. Should I tell her that I thought there had been money battles between Andy and Evan? I didn't know that, though, did I?

How did Gram handle these things? I felt lost and frustrated and didn't know how to reconcile what I did know with what I should tell Elle. What if those weren't actually battles and I put up walls between her and Andy that kept them from finding out what had happened to Evan?

"I got the sense that he had to write a check that he didn't want to write," I said. "Someone seemed to want money from him, but I don't know who." There, that was politic. Given the emotion behind the event, chances were, it was Andy, but I wasn't going to go any further on that. Elle could make her own decisions and talk to who she wanted. Andy could either come up with the truth or lie to her.

"It doesn't seem like him, you know?" Elle said. She looked up, tears threatening to spill.

"Maybe someone else used his pen? While most impressions likely come from Evan because it was his pen, if someone else used it when they were really emotional, that could leave a different impression. Maybe someone owed him some money, and Evan lent them the pen for a check?"

I didn't believe that. I was making it up as I

went along, but it reminded me that I only got impressions. I didn't actually know the who behind the object or the full story of what was going on. If people were going to come to me to ask me to help them, I was going to need to communicate things that might have happened and not just what I thought had happened.

Elle nodded. She reached out for the pen and I gave it back to her.

"Thank you for doing that. I didn't even think. Mrs. Beauvoir never charged…"

I shook my head. No way was I going to charge for such services. I didn't even want people to know I had this psychic talent.

I showed her out, and when she was gone I leaned against the door. I felt, as Gram might have said, wrung out like a used dishcloth. I hadn't worked, but there had been something emotional about this particular reading that I wasn't used to.

Penelope Blue showed up and rubbed against my legs. I heard Daisy moving about the back of the house. Win was walking across the hall upstairs, probably about to head down.

I started to go back into the study, but my stomach knotted. Then I got chilled. Penelope Blue arched her back and disappeared.

As I stood there, I felt cold, like the air from a freezer had just reached me and was wrapping itself around me. The room began to look a bit misty.

I had seen Gram's ghost and this was not how it happened at all. My heart began to beat faster while I tried to figure out what was going on.

Chapter 7

The sounds from the house faded as I watched the mist swirl in Gram's study. I backed up a few feet but I couldn't stop staring. I worried what would happen if I turned my back on the mist. I wanted to call out, but my voice stuck in my throat.

I clutched my shirt, wishing I was wearing something I loved that could ground me back into memories of things I loved. Instead, this was just a blouse that I liked, that I didn't have any emotional attachment to. I smelled a faint scent of red wine, as if someone were swirling a glass under my nose.

"Help me," a voice said.

The mist retreated and it was gone.

I frowned. Could it have been Evan Mabry

trying to reach me? After all, I'd just done a reading on him. Or was it someone else? I had no way of knowing. The hallway around me warmed again. I heard Win singing softly to herself as she reached the bottom of the stairs.

Daisy had turned on the television and was sitting down to watch it. All normal. Except Penelope Blue didn't normally arch her back and act as if she were about to hiss. I bit my lower lip and went upstairs.

It wasn't unusual for me to go up to the room I used. Morgan had tried to say that I should have the big bedroom with the en suite that Gram had, but I couldn't sleep there. Daisy had also refused it, taking a smaller room across the hall from Gram's. We were on opposite sides of the landing, though, so we each had our own shared bathroom.

Because we'd each refused to use Gram's room, it had been pretty much left as it was. Morgan and Win dusted and vacuumed, but the room itself remained as Gram had had it most of her life. It was one of the darker rooms in the house, done in green and brown and faded old floral wallpaper. If anyone had any doubts about the house's history, all they had to do was enter Gram's room and see that it really was old. She'd redone a lot of things, and the en suite was to die for.

I didn't need to use her lovely bathroom. I was looking for something of hers to touch, to bring me back to people that I knew and loved, and maybe, just maybe I'd see her ghost again.

I had once touched some earrings, thinking of her, and Gram had appeared. She wasn't a ghost that time. It was almost as if I'd caught an impression of her as a young woman, bringing her forward in time.

I'd prefer to see her ghost, but maybe the young woman would know enough to explain to me what had happened.

I stood before Gram's dressing table, an old-fashioned type of thing that had an oval mirror and a couple of small drawers to hold small toiletries and makeup. Gram had a tall jewelry box that sat in the closet, but there was a small box sitting on the dressing table that held her favorite jewelry pieces.

I picked up a small framed photo of Penelope Blue. The colors were fading from age. Penelope Blue's eyes, a deep Siamese blue, looked out from the shadows inside the silver metal frame. Gram had loved that cat.

Whenever I touched something of Gram's, it was automatic for me to shield myself from any sort of impression, so I had to consciously open myself, pretending to open a mental door to let in the impressions of what was happening.

I saw Gram as a young woman holding a very small Penelope Blue. The chocolate point Siamese was small and lithe and squirmed a little. Penelope Blue then reached up a paw to touch Gram's face before reaching up to lick Gram's chin. Gram giggled and petted her and then let the cat down. I didn't recognize the room Gram was in, but she often redid rooms.

I felt the joy Gram felt in the cat. Penelope Blue wasn't her first Siamese, but she was the one who endeared herself to Gram. Her face was more wedge shaped than the earlier cats, and Gram had found that interesting. Penelope Blue was also more wild, which was something Gram had appreciated. I got the sense that Gram felt the cat approved of her, too, and the two became good buddies.

The memory made laughter bubble up inside me. There was sadness too, when Penelope Blue had gotten older. There were plenty of other memories in between of an adult cat sunning herself, washing her belly, of Gram coming upon the cat hidden under the blankets on a cold evening.

I pulled myself out, wishing I had known my grandmother as a younger woman. I set the frame down, hoping that when I turned around a young Gram would be seated behind me. My fingers lingered on the frame, remembering how she'd just appeared after I let go of the earrings last time.

Maybe if I kept that thought in mind, she'd be there, on the bed, once again.

I let go of the silver frame reluctantly, setting it carefully back down in its place. Win was very good about making sure everything stayed neat and tidy. She didn't want anyone messing with Gram's things without letting her know. I turned slowly towards the bed, expectations high.

The bed was empty. Not even the ghost of Penelope Blue, who often appeared to me. I waited.

I listened for any odd sounds, but all I heard was a particularly loud laugh from what I gathered was a commercial on the television downstairs. I smelled nothing unusual. There was no sense of waiting, no sense that anything was going to happen. Only my own hope that was fading quickly.

I had so hoped I could talk to Gram. I didn't know who else I could talk to about ghosts and weird things. Daisy and Morgan may know about my talent, but they didn't know how it worked. They also didn't know that it included seeing ghosts—well, human ghosts. They knew about Penelope Blue.

Had this experience been a ghost sighting or something else?

Given that I had no one else to talk to, I decided to hunt around the internet to see what I could find.

I headed over to the room I was using. I liked this room because it had a large window that looked over the front driveway and the trees out there. I could see if anyone came up the drive, too. At some point a desk had been built into the corner next to the small walk-in closet. That gave me a private place to work. I did most of my work at the office, but if I needed to do something on the computer, I wanted to have privacy to do so.

The healthcare privacy laws were very strict, so I made sure I was honoring them.

I settled in at the white desk, using the straight-backed chair. There wasn't quite room for an office chair. I found it cozy though sometimes I missed being able to spread out on the little desk I'd purchased for the eating area in the carriage house.

I searched out white mists and ghosts. While there were plenty of legends, there wasn't any good stuff. I moved on to legends about white mists in the Seales area. Again, I struck out. I decided to search Evan Mabry's name.

I did find an article about him disappearing. His husband, Andy Willard, was said to be concerned that Evan hadn't turned up. There was no mention of Elle.

The article wasn't nearly as informative as I

would have liked. I sat and drummed my fingers against the desk, wondering what I ought to do next. Cheri might have information, but that would entail telling her about reading objects. I wasn't quite ready to do that, though given that Elle might talk, I should work on fessing up to Cheri sooner rather than later.

I wasn't sure what the mists meant and without Gram to help me, I had no idea what to do next. Hopefully this was a one-time thing. I really didn't want to get dragged into something weird just because I read an object for a stranger who came begging at my door.

I sighed, thinking I watched too many horror stories. Now all I could think about was an evil spirit attached to Gram's house. That wasn't comforting. It was even worse because Penelope Blue didn't immediately show up to curl up on the desk. I mean, usually she only showed up if she thought I needed to pay attention to something, but still, the little ghost cat was quite a comfort. Though the door was open, Hellspark and Babs also left me to my own devices.

At least I didn't have to worry about them being devoured by supernatural forces. That was something, at least. Not something particularly comforting, but something.

Chapter 8

Friday, the day after I found the body of Layla Wiltshire, I got ready to go into work a bit earlier than usual. No one had called to tell me I couldn't use my office, so I hoped things were better. I had tossed and turned all night, trying to remind myself that if the voice in the mist was really evil, it wasn't likely to go around saying, "Help me."

Fortunately, Daisy didn't comment on the dark bags under my eyes when I had some tea and toast with her that morning. Win was in the kitchen. Morgan was puttering about the downstairs cleaning things. He knew about Gram's talent and knew about mine, having suspected it when Gram insisted upon leaving me the house. I wondered if he noticed anything unusual in Gram's study. At least if I asked him, I wouldn't have to explain what I meant by unusual.

It would have to wait because I had a patient coming in at ten. I wanted to be sure there weren't any restrictions on my office that morning, and if there were, I needed time to contact my patient. That meant an early morning for me.

The day was dawning clear with the temperature rising. We'd likely have thunderstorms in the afternoon. Like yesterday, I had patients in the morning, but none later in the day. Friday afternoons tended to be either very busy or not busy at all, and it was impossible to predict which.

I turned onto the road that ran by the grocery store, surprised at how busy it was. I turned into my lot and parked in my usual spot. There were more cars there than I would have expected. I walked around the front, making sure all was well. No crime scene tape blocked the area, though there were a few pieces fluttering around the edges of the parking lot.

My massage therapist, Pam, was there talking to Colleen, who was the front office person at the chiropractor's. Duncan Sparks, the chiropractor, was out there too, along with Deena Reynolds, who ran the pizza place. Even Piers Leeson, who ran the tax place, was standing out front, looking uncomfortable about all the human contact. Piers may be a good tax preparer but he's not a people person.

"Morning, Ash!" Pam called. Pam is tall and willowy and nearing forty. She's been doing massage for almost a decade, and she's starting to worry about her wrists and arms. Part of working for me means I give her regular acupuncture at no charge. It was her idea, but I didn't care. It was good PR. Given what had happened to Marty, I needed all the goodwill I could get.

Colleen grinned, which is sort of second nature to her. As always, her short blonde hair was a perfect little helmet surrounding her round face.

Duncan turned and nodded at me. He always holds himself a little apart, no matter that he tries to dress down in jeans and a button-down shirt. He always looks like he should be in a suit, no matter that he does a fairly physical job when he adjusts.

Deena gave me a wave, taking a step towards me. Plump and round, just the sort of person you want making your pizzas, Deena was the oldest of us, her hair going gray and her face lined.

"Morning," I said as I got closer. They were all standing around in front of the big windows of my office that said, "Ash Jericho, Acupuncture and Herbs." I'd had someone paint the window so that it looked nice and was readable when you were in the front parking lot where it was hard to see the sign above on the roof. We all had signage up there and it was great advertising for those driving by down on the highway.

"It must have been horrible for you yesterday," Colleen said, shuddering. It was a little theatrical on her part.

"I didn't even realize she was dead at first," I said. "That was creepy."

Duncan nodded. "Too bad for her. It's horrible that it was by your office when she seemed to have a thing against having you here doing herbs —legally, I might add."

"I heard she just gave herbs and stuff," I said, tentatively. If she wasn't taking money, I wasn't sure where that fell in practicing medicine without a license.

"She overstepped boundaries quite a bit," Duncan said. "She took money for her herbs, recommended patients not take medications given by doctors, that sort of thing. She had quite a reputation among local providers. From my perspective, as a doctor in the community, you couldn't have gotten better PR as far as getting professional referrals, than Layla badmouthing you."

I felt Duncan was overstating the case a bit. It wasn't as if chiropractors were all held in high esteem among medical doctors, not in Kentucky. The idea that he was on the same footing as a medical doctor was rather amusing. I didn't want to diss Duncan's achievements, but he tended towards a certain level of pomposity.

"We lost all the lunch crowd," Deena said. "I know it sounds horrible, but it worried me because we get a fair number in with our buy a slice, get one free Thursdays. Course, I expect the goons will all be in today once they know for sure we're back open."

"When did the police leave?" I asked.

"Seven or eight last night," Deena said. "They let us open, but people had to stay way back and park in the grocery store, so a lot thought we were still closed. Might as well have been."

"My patient called to be sure I was able to be here," Pam said. "I told her I'd check to be sure I could be. I just texted her a little bit before you arrived."

"I was checking, too." I glanced around, looking at things.

"Layla was one of my customers," Piers said quietly. "She was nice enough to me but not to my staff. Nothing they ever did was right. I had to go over all her returns myself, and she'd only deal with me, not even my wife when she worked reception during the busy season."

That seemed par for the course from Layla.

"I think about the only person who might have liked her was Gina Jakes over at the produce stand on the Seales By-Pass," Deena said.

Gina ran a small farm, mostly vegetables, and sold them at a little farm stand over on the By-Pass. If I remembered correctly, she also sold some of Layla's herbs.

"Didn't she sell Layla's herbs too?" I asked.

Duncan nodded. "Sold pretty well out there, although to be honest, they were mostly kitchen type herbs that she sold, not the medicinal ones. Still, it seemed to work well for both of them."

"I admit she wasn't very nice," Colleen said, "but it's just so hard to believe that anyone would just up and murder her. And here in our parking lot. I know it was in between Ash and Deena's places, but that could point the finger at any of us. It's not like she was very nice to anyone here."

Which I suppose meant that I was standing in a group of suspects. Unfortunately, I had no idea how to go about ruling anyone out. I knew everyone there and while I didn't love them, I liked them well enough. Deena was real sweet and she'd talked to me about wanting me to help her stop smoking a few times, but never quite came in. She wasn't smoking then, though I had a feeling she wanted to light up. It was something she tried to avoid doing right outside her front door.

Piers was quiet and uncomfortable around

people, at least in groups. Still, if you needed someone for tax help and you didn't need a full accountant, he was honest and above board. He was also fairly generous with his time if you got over his inability to really chat and the fact that he never looked you in the eye.

Honestly, as far as Piers was concerned, I saw him getting murdered rather than being the murderer.

Duncan was a bit full of himself and Colleen was a little bit over nice. She'd been Duncan's receptionist for the last five years. Before that, she'd worked for the same dentist Marty had worked at. She'd been quite nice when Marty had died and had been one of those people who let me know she'd never believed I could harm my cousin.

I hadn't known Pam from before, but her recommendations as a massage therapist had been glowing. She worked part time up in Frankfort for another acupuncturist that I had a lot of respect for. I couldn't imagine that there was anything in her background.

I realized then that I was running through people I knew, friends even, and seeing if they fit the bill for being a murderer. I couldn't believe I was thinking like that. I needed to leave suspicion to the police and not take it on myself.

I shook my head as I went to unlock my office.

Looking through the window that closely, I realized that I couldn't see the top edge of the black computer monitor that I had on the reception desk. My stomach started to sink. Not something else.

Chapter 9

I have to admit that my hands shook as I opened the lock, hoping that somehow I was just missing something as I looked through the glass. I got inside to see that no, there was no computer on the desk behind the neat little window I had to separate it from the waiting area.

"Pam," I said. "My computer appears to be gone."

Pam came in immediately, followed by everyone else. That many people in my little waiting room made it feel overcrowded. Everyone was touching the door as they came in. I had touched the door. If anyone had left prints, we'd never find them now. Of course, what was I thinking? No one would find prints on a public door anyway.

I looked around. Everything else seemed to be in place. I had furnished my office with armless chairs and a low table from IKEA. I had a selection of women's magazines I purchased just for the office. I had subscribed to National Geographic, but so far only two issues had arrived. They were all laid out in a fan on the low table and everything seemed in order. The space smelled faintly of herbs.

The crush of bodies lent itself to the sounds of fabric brushing against fabric and the stray growl of a stomach. No one was talking. I felt them waiting for me to find something, to say something.

I hurried through the door to the reception area and looked around. My computer was a full PC with a box, not that fancy. In fact, you could purchase something like it for little enough considering I didn't intend to use it for anything but inputting inventory and doing patient records. Most of that was online, so I thought I was okay as far HIPAA. I had password protected the thing with a twenty-digit string. Byron may not be involved in computer crimes, but he knew enough to make sure I kept my system as safe as I could.

The computer box was in its place. The screen was on the floor, turned on. It was asking for a password. I knew I hadn't done it. The fact that the screen was on suggested that someone had been there moments ago. They had probably heard us and fled out the back as I rattled the door trying to fit my key in the lock.

If I hadn't talked to anyone, maybe I would have seen someone going out the back. They had to have gone out that way, right?

"It's down here on the floor," I whispered.

Duncan put a finger to his lips. He gestured to the rest of us to wait in the reception area.

I watched as he made large goose step tip-toes like he was in an old Saturday morning cartoon marching up behind someone. Most people would have looked silly doing that, but somehow this worked for Duncan. Not a single board creaked on the floor, which was slightly unusual, as he made his way to the first room.

He paused and glanced inside quickly.

He straightened and looked back at me, shaking his head.

The goose stepping continued as Duncan made his way down the hall. The next door was on the left. He poked his head in there too. Moments later he was again shaking his head.

The last door was Pam's room. This door was closed, which was normal.

Duncan reached it, raising his eyebrows looking from me to Pam.

I shrugged. I didn't know for certain the door

had been closed the night before, but chances were it was.

Duncan opened that door slowly, hoping to avoid a creak. Fortunately, I worried about noises in my office, and the door was quiet. He peered inside but apparently saw no one.

Walking a bit more easily, Duncan looked in the back office. He even stepped inside, but apparently saw no one.

Finally he was ready to check the bathroom. That door was closed too. Oddly polite, Duncan knocked first. I wasn't sure why, but perhaps the idea of knocking on a bathroom door was too much of an ingrained habit.

Duncan turned the knob slowly. It seemed to take him forever to open the door, pushing it only partway open, far enough to let him look inside.

Shaking his head, Duncan started back down the hallway, walking normally now.

He was perhaps halfway to the front when I saw a shadow behind him. It formed into a darkly clothed human as it emerged from the bathroom.

"He's there!" I called, but the outside door was already open.

The shadow person was already running outside.

I moved to give chase.

Duncan hurried back down the hallway. He

didn't run very fast and he was big enough that I couldn't push past him.

Frustrated, I hurried along behind him.

Unfortunately, by the time we got to the back door, the person was gone. My intruder could have been hiding behind a dumpster, waiting to attack, or they could be across the way in the grocery store parking lot, hiding behind a car or maybe blending in with the innocent shoppers. I didn't see anyone in all black, but if they were wearing a jacket, they could have pulled it off.

"Well, we know your intruder was fast," Duncan said.

"Why look at the computer?" I asked.

No one had an answer. I wondered what the intruder had been looking for. I went up front and searched through my purse. I grabbed my cell phone and dialed the non-emergency police number. After all, no one was in my office except for the people I had brought with me.

I couldn't help but think this incident was related to what had happened to Layla.

Pam talked to Duncan and the others while I talked to the police dispatcher. She assured me she'd send someone by. I hoped that someone was not Gil Daffney. I did not want to have to work with him any further. Of course, perhaps seeing this was potential theft, Byron could come by.

I listened to the voices around me. Someone

left, probably Deena from the fact that there was less laughter when the door closed.

I looked at the small black computer mouse sitting on the desk with the keyboard. Only the screen was on the floor. An awkward angle to have been typing and watching, but it would have kept someone's head low.

I wondered if I could get any impressions from the mouse. I might mess up fingerprints if they hadn't used gloves. But they'd been dressed in dark clothing, ready to flee if someone came in. They had probably worn gloves. Still, I decided to touch the back of the mouse where there were least likely to be fingerprints.

The mouse was cool beneath my fingers, not at all like something that someone had just used. I had to consciously let go of my guardedness to open to impressions.

I got a sense of slight worry, of hope. That was me. I saw myself in my last office, an old building in Vancouver, Washington, just across the river from Portland, Oregon. It was a cheery place with lots of sunshine and plants and plenty of people. I wanted the same kind of thing for this space even if it wasn't as nicely appointed.

I felt my own sense of concern, of frustration, of actual fear of how I'd be perceived by the local community. Then, overlaying that was something else. A sense of frustration, of not being able to get the information wanted.

Evan's name shot into my mind. The idea that he might have come here. There was the need to know when.

There was a certainty that he'd been here as a patient. It was only a question of when. The certainty was at such odds with what I knew, that I was thrown out of the trance.

I hadn't seen him, so why would someone be sure that I had? Did this have to do with Layla?

As I stood, I realized that if someone didn't know better, they might think that Pam used my office computer as well. She sometimes used it to log onto her online scheduler, but she kept nothing on this system. Could she have treated Evan Mabry?

I'd have to talk to her. Maybe she could shed some light on what was going on. I mean, I didn't expect her to break patient confidentiality, but seeing Elle had visited me and I knew Evan was missing, I could at least broach the subject.

I drew in a breath feeling better, feeling as if a few pieces were falling into place. The bigger picture was still a mess, but I thought I might be making sense of what I did know.

"Did they give you a time?" Colleen asked, looking at me, her eyes large.

I shook my head. "She just said she was sending someone."

"Hopefully not that Daffney guy," Piers said. "He's got an attitude problem. In my day, the police understood they worked for us."

Duncan was nodding at Piers. So Daffney hadn't just ruffled my feathers. Too bad Seales couldn't hire police people actually liked.

"Too bad the nice Detective Cabot wasn't officially on the case," Colleen said. "He's very polite. And that young man they hired a few years back, Roy Newman. He usually works the downtown area, but he is a nice fellow. Very helpful."

Piers and Duncan agreed and started talking about their interactions, all on the side of the law, of course, with the various police officers in Seales. I had to admit they seemed to run into police with an unnerving frequency based on their stories.

I heard a car outside and Colleen looked up, surprised. "I have to get going!" she sang as she hurried through the door.

Duncan looked out as well and announced he had to get to work. He didn't move with any hurry, confident that his patient would be willing to wait while he finished talking to Piers.

Once he was the only one left, Piers also decided to leave. I thought that was fortunate, given I didn't know what to say to him. I watched him go around by the pizza place. Had he put in an early order?

I didn't see him go back past, though I was watching the window for the police, hoping they'd get there before I had my patient.

I wondered what Piers was doing there if he wasn't going to his office. I was getting far too nosey and suspicious.

Pam's morning person arrived moments later, so I didn't have a chance to ask Pam about Evan. Instead, I huddled alone behind the reception desk. My fingers tapped the counter and my brain worked overtime trying to figure out why all this was happening to me.

Finally, I saw a police car drive up. Byron got out, which made me relax but only for a moment. His mouth was set in a line and he did not look happy to be there.

Chapter 10

I stood up, waiting for Byron to walk to the office. He looked around the parking lot, as if searching for anyone who appeared out of place. Normally, with the pizza place next door, just about anyone would fit in. It was early enough that there wouldn't be many visitors to Deena's, though I knew people often ordered early to take out.

I watched as Byron walked slowly across the blacktop on the lot, still scanning the area. He pushed open the door to my office, making the bell ring just a little. I had about fifteen minutes before my patient was due to arrive. I hoped this wouldn't take long.

"What happened?" he asked.

Even from there, I smelled peppermint from a

mint he was chewing on. I had a moment to wonder if he'd been drinking, but I hadn't known Byron to ever drink to excess. Besides, it was barely past breakfast time. Sometimes a mint is just a mint.

"I got here a bit early, to make sure I wouldn't have to direct my morning patient in through the back," I said. I described meeting everyone in front, talking a bit, though I left out that we were second guessing who might have killed Layla. No sense in making Byron any more miffed than he already was.

I realized that as a burglary, this was the sort of call he normally wouldn't have answered. Normally that went to patrol.

"When I unlocked the door, I noticed that my computer screen wasn't there. I can usually see just the top edge of it through the reception window. I went inside to see if I were mistaken. I found the screen sitting on the floor. I noticed it was still on—it hadn't gone to black like it does when it hasn't been used for a while—and then Duncan Sparks, the chiropractor from down the way, searched the place. He didn't see anyone, but he didn't look very hard."

Byron was making notes, not looking at me much. In fact, he was barely looking at me at all.

"As soon as Duncan was almost back to the reception area, someone hurried out of the bathroom. They fled through the back door. Duncan tried to go after him. So did I, but we didn't get out of here fast enough." I wanted to add that Duncan didn't move very fast. Had he gone slowly on purpose?

I mean, chances were, I could have run fast enough to have tackled the intruder, but I hadn't been able to get by Duncan. He'd almost purposely blocked me. Had it been a sense of chivalry or perhaps his own sense of importance that made him keep me from passing him and catching the intruder, or had he had another reason?

"And that's all? Nothing was taken? The computer screen was moved?"

"Not that I've noticed. But someone broke in," I said. I did not mention Evan Mabry's name. "I was concerned after what happened to Layla Wiltshire."

Concerned did not even begin to state how I really felt, but it sounded good to my ears.

Byron gave a few nods and walked around. He looked at the computer and made a note. He did not reach down to check anything.

"Are you going to check for prints?" I asked.

Byron looked at me then and frowned. "No."

I frowned. "Why not?"

"Nothing is missing. And it's a public place. Your reception area is off limits, but I could have reached over and touched the monitor when it was on the desk from here. So could any of your patients. If you've ever had cleaning people in, they could have touched it. We'll waste taxpayer dollars and get a ton of useless prints when all that happened was that someone broke in." Byron waited for me to fight him on that.

I shrugged. Not that it mattered, given I had touched the mouse, but I had been so careful to try not to mess up fingerprints.

"Why are you answering this call?" I asked. "I thought you mostly did major crimes. This isn't even big enough to warrant paying for fingerprints."

"Given that, once again, you are somewhat involved with a local major crime, I've been relegated to answering these sorts of calls. At least I don't have to go on patrol," Byron said.

"I'm sorry." I really was. It wasn't like I planned these things.

"It's not your fault," Byron said. He gave me a half smile. So he wasn't completely angry with me. He was just frustrated with his life. That made me feel a little better.

"I wish these things wouldn't happen to me," I agreed. "It's not like I like being part of an investigation. Officer Daffney certainly seemed to think I had plenty of motive."

Byron shook his head. "He's an idiot. He's newer on the force and thinks he knows it all. We only have a few people with experience, and so the younger guys often get paired together and they feed off each other."

"Do you think Layla's murder was related to one of these businesses?" I asked.

"Hard to say," Byron said, loosening up a little. I hoped he'd be more forthcoming than that.

"It's doubtful she was murdered in your parking lot. There wasn't any blood. Either someone did a stunning job cleaning up—hard to do when the highway is just there—or someone brought her here and posed her. What I don't know is if she was there for you to find or if she was just placed here for someone else to find and you got unlucky."

I nodded my agreement. Everything Byron said was true. I hadn't even noticed the lack of blood. Some detective I would be.

"I'd ask you for dinner tomorrow," Byron said, "but the station is frowning on me continuing to pursue a relationship with someone who is a potential suspect."

I tried to smile, but it annoyed me. A potential suspect, though. That was better than being a full suspect. And Officer Daffney wasn't planting himself outside my home like Clair Wilcox had. Of course, after what happened to her, if Daffney had believed anything he said, he wouldn't have chanced being there.

"It would have been nice. All the more reason for this murder to get tied up, isn't it?" I tried to make light of the situation.

Byron agreed, giving me a half smile.

He was about to leave when my next patient came in. Sandra Fletcher is a petite woman a few years older than I am. She was prone to stress and complained of migraines. She'd been doing so much better with acupuncture.

"Byron!" Sandra smiled, reaching for him. "Why did you come here? We could have talked later."

I watched as Byron started to blush.

Suddenly my stomach felt weird and my shoulders tensed. There wasn't any reason for Byron not to know Sandra, but there was something intimate in the way she seemed to have expected to see him. Even that could have been explained. What got me was the blush. I hadn't ever seen Byron blush before.

As my stomach started turning out butterflies and I had to process what kind of relationship the two might have, I realized the last thing I wanted to have to do was treat Sandra, but it was exactly what my job entailed. I breathed in, hoping to calm myself, trying to pretend I wasn't going to listen to the rest of their conversation.

Chapter 11

Byron looked down at the ground and then back at Sandra. He was trying to act normal, but I could see the tension in his shoulders, which matched my own.

The office suddenly felt too small. Even though I was behind a partial wall, I felt stifled and wanted to get out of there. The herbal smell seemed too much, and I wanted to run outside and sniff the clean, clear air, free from anything that reminded me of my home. If Byron was confronting another girlfriend—is that appropriate for adults?—or whatever, I didn't want it to happen in my place or in front of me.

I waited, listening to my heartbeat, for the next words.

"Ash had an apparent break-in. I got the call

to check it out." Byron stood puffing his chest just a bit, as if he dared Sandra to say something.

"I didn't know you did that sort of investigation. Particularly with a murder nearby so recently," Sandra said. She gave Byron a hard stare, the sort that Gram would give when she knew someone was lying.

Byron just shrugged. He looked at me, not too long, but merely a glance, before saying, "I'll contact you if we find anything."

I nodded, hoping I didn't break any of the teeth while I clenched my jaw.

While it might have soothed my own ego to give him a hard time, I needed to be fresh and nice for Sandra. I didn't need to bring any hurt feelings into the office, not if I could help it. I tried to remember if Sandra had talked about seeing anyone. I knew she was single and that she wasn't happy about it.

"Come on back," I said. I always leave the rooms clean before leaving. I was glad of that because I hadn't even considered going back and checking. I hoped that if my intruder had left a mess anywhere, Duncan would have said something.

I led Sandra into the first room, the one I rarely use, because I knew it was the cleanest. If I had missed something yesterday when I was distracted, or today when I was even more distracted, it wouldn't be apparent in this room.

"I haven't been in here before," Sandra said.

"The last couple of days have been busy," I said, seating myself. Sandra was in a low chair that allowed her to sit comfortably. It had no arms so anyone of any size would fit. The treatment table wasn't as fancy as the one in the other room, which was an electric model that raised and lowered and I could adjust it for someone who needed a sitting position or have it lie flat. While I loved it, those tables were expensive. I could afford a second one, but I didn't want to spend all my money setting up a practice if it couldn't at least support itself.

Instead, in this room, I had a regular massage table that was extra sturdy and wide. Cream flannel sheets covered it. While it was a bit more work for patients to climb up on, they'd feel safe and secure once there.

"I heard about Layla." Sandra leaned forward a little as she spoke, her dark hair swinging across her face slightly. She had very straight hair, and I wondered how long it took her to get that look in the morning. Her eyes were blue and she had a pretty smile. I don't normally judge my patients as far as their attractiveness, but after the incident with Byron, I found myself wondering if he found her pretty.

"It was a shock," I admitted.

Sandra nodded. "I'm surprised that Byron was here about a break-in. I would have thought it was about the murder. He's a detective, you know."

"I know," I said. "I talked with him when my cousin was killed. Why don't we move on to how you are?"

Sandra wanted to say something else. She chewed her lip before letting the moment pass and started telling me about her week. She'd not had a single headache, for which she was pleased. I suspected that next week we'd see more because that had been her pattern for the last few treatments. The headaches weren't as bad, though, which was always a good sign.

I drew Sandra through the intake, finding out what else had been going on. She said nothing about seeing anyone or problems in a relationship, not that my intake asks anything like that directly. There are plenty of places where such things can come up, like when I ask about stress.

When I left her to undress and get comfortable for treatment, I took several deep breaths, trying to calm my mind so that I could focus on her. I hated feeling off balance when I began a treatment. The last couple of days had been horrible for that. At least yesterday, with Ryan, the stress had been external to him.

I inserted Sandra's needles and then came back out of the room. I moved the computer monitor back to where it needed to be. I was surprised to see that I had to unplug the screen and keyboard to get that to work properly. Someone had taken some time to move the thing to the floor.

They'd have had almost as much time leaving it on the desk and searching for something, keeping their head down. Moving the monitor made no sense to me. I sat at the desk, trying to see what might have spoken to an intruder, but there was nothing obvious.

I texted Cheri to let her know what had happened. I hadn't talked to her since the day before. She might have some more gossip about Layla's murder. I really wanted to talk to her to see if she could find out anything about Byron's private life. I couldn't ask her directly about Sandra because of patient confidentiality, but I could certainly ask about Byron.

Granted, Cheri had been trying to get that information for the last six months. Just because no one knew he was seeing someone didn't mean he wasn't. Or something like that.

I input Sandra's billing information into the computer. By the time I finished, I could go pull needles. Pam came out of her treatment room, talking to her patient. I hoped she'd stick around for a bit. I wanted to ask about Evan Mabry. I just needed to figure out how to bring it up.

Everything went smoothly while I got Sandra charged out. She even set up another appointment. It shouldn't have surprised me, but I worried that somehow she was aware of the tension between Byron and me and that would make it awkward for us. Apparently, it was just awkward for me.

Pam was just finishing changing her sheets and putting them in a basket.

"When's your next one?" I asked.

"I was supposed to have Erik, but he called and cancelled. Had to work," Pam said. "I get an hour break to go over my books. Lucky me."

"I was wondering," I said, trying to be casual, "I ran into Elle Mabry and she was talking about how her son Evan had gone missing. You've worked around here forever. Did you know him?"

Pam nodded. "I've met Elle several times, too. Evan was a good friend. It's been horrible having him gone. Andy is ripped up."

"I haven't met Andy," I said, hoping she wouldn't ask how I knew Evan, considering I didn't, except through a pen that his mother had given me.

Again, with the smile. "Andy is the sweetest guy. He's always got something going on. Right now, he wants to work as a chef. He has a great job over in Lexington as a sous chef. He's fantastic with food. I love going over there to eat. I can't believe Evan didn't immediately invite you over. Ever since they got together, he's all about showing Andy off!"

I just smiled, hoping to let that slide. I never actually said I knew Evan, just Elle.

"I mostly know Elle," I said.

"That's right," Pam said. "Elle is kind of a piece of work. She's been trying to break Evan and Andy up since they got together. She threatened to not go to the wedding. Broke Evan's heart with the threat. I'm not sure what he would have done if she hadn't ended up going. Too many people thought it was because she didn't approve of her son marrying a man, any man, not just Andy. Turns out she didn't like that gossip."

"That's hard when families don't like who you're dating."

"Tell mc about it. It's Sandra's problem, too." Pam suddenly changed the subject, surprising me. "Even when she meets someone, her family tends to dislike them. They like to think they're old money, but they aren't really. Her dad just got lucky in the stock market when Sandra was a teenager. Suddenly, they decided she needed a rich husband. She'd have been after Byron in a heartbeat if he had a better job."

"I had no idea," I said. So that was the connection.

"To tell the truth, I think she's considered leaving the area just so she could be with who she wanted to be. Byron's pretty planted, though, and I think Sandra would really only be happy if she could leave with him. Poor woman, damned if she stays, damned if she goes. So, instead she lives here and lets everyone tell her what to do, which stresses her out."

"You do seem quite informed," I said.

"Her family is from Frankfort like mine, so I know her. I'm less knowledgeable about all the families here in Seales."

I realized I didn't know where the Mabrys lived. I couldn't ask Pam now without giving away that I didn't really know them. The internet would probably help me with that information, though.

I went back to working on the computer while Pam worked on her stuff. I had no other patients that day, so I could leave whenever.

Just as I was about to go, Cheri answered my text with one of her own. I was surprised to see that she thought I needed to get to the coffee shop immediately. Given that I was thinking about leaving anyway, I said goodbye to Pam and grabbed my stuff.

Chapter 12

It didn't take me long to get to the coffee shop, but when I walked in, Cheri was bouncing around as if she'd been waiting hours. The place smelled wonderfully of coffee and chocolate. Soft music played in the background. The old building, with its uncovered brick walls, created a nice cozy atmosphere with chintz chairs, ruffled curtains tied back over the blinds, and a wood floor that looked unfinished. The counter where Cheri served coffee and sweet treats was scarred and worn. The place hadn't changed since shabby chic had come into fashion. Apparently, here it never left.

I wasn't sure why Cheri appeared so impatient with me. She knew my office was out on the highway a good ten minutes away from downtown

Seales. It was a direct shot, but it still took time unless I was going to race through the streets and ignore a few stop signs. We'd all done that when we were kids. Now, I was old enough to know better, especially when, as an acupuncturist, I often saw the aftermath of some of those accidents.

"What's up?" I asked, going up to her station. Cheri was pulling drinks, but fortunately there was a lull.

"See that guy over there." Cheri pointed out an older man with gray hair and the beginnings of a beard. He was heavyset, wearing a pair of faded overalls. He could have been the muscle on a bad TV show about Appalachia.

I nodded, looking back at her.

"That's Harry O'Reilly."

I waited. The name didn't really ring a bell.

"Layla's place backs up to his farm. She had some land, but not enough to call it a farm, you know," Cheri said. It's really amazing how many words she can get in without taking a breath.

"Ah," I said.

"He told me that she'd been worried about something for a few days. Asked him to look in on her property and everything and, get this, she even wanted to him to feed her dog if something happened to her. Can you imagine what she was thinking if she was going so far as to ask someone for that kind of help? I asked him if she said why she was worried, but he didn't tell me, and I thought that maybe if you were here you could sit down and chat with him," Cheri said.

I had to take a breath after that speech. Cheri seemed perfectly fine.

"He doesn't even know me," I said.

Cheri shrugged. "He's just sitting there by himself. He comes in every two weeks for a coffee and just sits. No one ever talks to him even though he's lived here forever. I feel kind of bad."

I glared. I was just supposed to sit down and make conversation with an old man that I didn't know. I didn't even have a coffee to act like I belonged.

Cheri read my mind on that last one as she handed me a tall, plain coffee. It's not my favorite, but I wasn't paying. How could I complain? It clearly solved the problem of why I might be sitting down in the shop.

I took it, sniffed it, let the smell perk me up a bit. I was so nervous that perhaps perking me up wasn't what I actually needed. I took the moment to gather my thoughts and calm my pounding heart.

I walked over to the table near where Harry was sitting. I set my coffee down and pawed through my purse as if I were looking for my phone.

Harry didn't say anything though he noticed.

He just kept on drinking. He wasn't using a phone.

I pulled out my phone and looked at a few names. Then I set it down while I took a seat. "Morning."

Harry looked over at me and nodded. Great. He wasn't a talker.

I wondered if he'd be better off if I took a direct tack or if I should continue to sit there.

"You that Beauvoir girl?" he asked.

"My mom was a Beauvoir, but I'm a Jericho," I said. At least he was striking up a conversation.

"Layla was killed out by your place, wasn't she?"

I nodded.

"Suppose you're wondering what I know." Harry picked up his coffee and took a drink. His face was oval and he looked very placid and calm. His eyes had an intelligent gleam that suggested he was used to being underestimated, though.

"I'd love to know it, seeing she died outside my office. Naturally that puts all of us as suspects." That way he wouldn't think that I was being singled out as a suspect. So far as I knew, I wasn't. Still, I'd learned to be wary.

"Puts you in a pickle, again. Heard you were suspected of your cousin's death, too."

Harry was far too well informed.

"We did find the killer," I said, "although several other people died before the police found him. It was a very tragic time."

"You think you know more than the cops?"

"I'm wondering if maybe Layla was trying to find me to let me know something. My office was broken into this morning. It makes me think that maybe she was trying to warn me about something. I realize she didn't like what I did, so it must have been something really important." Okay, now the spin was coming. I mentally patted myself on the back for the way I put that.

"She was kind of weirded out about something," Harry said. "Don't know what it was, but she was certainly worried. Even asked me to feed her dog if something happened."

"I can't believe she didn't tell anyone what she was worried about," I said. "Did she have anyone she'd confide in?"

"Layla was…" Harry looked up at the ceiling as if he were searching for a word. He paused for a long time, licking his lips. Finally, "Self-sufficient. She did things herself, took pride in taking care of herself. Had been doing so as long as I knew her. She'd been around a good fifteen years, I think, give or take. Always growing her own food and what not. I know that's how she ended up getting into herbs. She wasn't nice, not even very polite all the time, not even with me. I'm not sure she meant to be difficult. It was more like she was because she didn't think being nice or tactful or anything would get her anywhere, not really."

I took a sip of my coffee, which was now cool enough that I could do so without burning my tongue off. Cheri was looking at me, eyebrows raised as if she wanted a report right then.

I smiled at her a little bit and looked back at Harry. "If you had to guess what had happened to her, what do you think happened?"

"She pissed off the wrong person."

"Any ideas on who?" I asked.

Harry shrugged and stared off into space. I played with my coffee, waiting for a better answer. As I started becoming more certain one wouldn't be forthcoming, he spoke.

"Can't say as I want to point fingers," Harry said. "There are too many to count, really. She pissed off a lot of folks. Even that nice woman who sells her herbs at her stand. Layla was out there saying she gave her more than she did and she was being short changed. Gina was real upset. Layla stays on the good side of Piers Leeson only because she said she worries he'll cheat on her taxes and get her in trouble if she doesn't. There aren't many other people who might be in a position to cause her trouble like that, so they all have reasons."

"Even you?" I asked.

Harry smiled. "There were days it could have

been, but I'm not a young man and I've learned to tolerate the neighbors. And I came to see she's a sad, sad woman."

Which were all things I knew, so while I had a few more names and a bit more detail, I hadn't actually learned anything new.

Harry sipped his coffee, still thinking.

I did the same. Cheri was about jumping up and down as if I should run over there and talk to her. I tried not to roll my eyes.

"There was that young man, named Andy or something. Think he might have been related to her distantly. Came around from time to time. Ain't seen him recently."

I was immediately put in mind of Andy Willard. Could they be one and the same?

Chapter 13

I actually sat and finished my coffee. Harry left without so much as a goodbye. I was surprised that he had talked to me at all. I felt as if he were just as strange as Layla, in his own way. But Harry, at least, seemed to have family and friends that he knew. He apparently thought that Layla didn't have anyone, except maybe himself and someone named Andy.

Andy wasn't a common name in Seales. Given that I had just heard it from Elle, I had to consider it wasn't a coincidence.

The music playing in the background had given way to a song that vaguely resembled something once popular which grated on my nerves. I felt as if I could get a headache if I listened much longer. The smell of coffee had receded. It was funny how quickly the room stopped being cozy and became dull when the coffee smell disappeared.

Cheri was motioning me over, not even acting like she was trying to be discrete any longer. I nodded. A heavyset woman with long dark hair was talking to the cashier. Cheri was going to be making a drink soon.

I walked over, having nothing else to do. I'd been sitting in one of the chintz chairs and I was surprised at how uncomfortable they were, at least for me. I hadn't even noticed until I stood up and felt almost as if my legs wouldn't move.

"Those chairs are nasty," I said.

Cheri nodded. "I'd have warned you to drag over one of the wooden ones, but that might have looked funny. Harry's the only one who ever uses those chairs unless they've never been in before."

"I certainly won't be using them again." I rubbed the side of my hip, wondering if I was going to need to give myself a treatment.

"So what did he say?" Cheri asked, picking up the cup that the cashier had passed. She looked at it and started making the drink, her hands quick and efficient at the machines, finding the ingredients with barely a glance. It was rather the way some women could knit, just looking now and then to be sure they were doing what they thought they should be.

"Just that lots of folks didn't like her," I said quietly. The heavyset woman was standing nearby, waiting on her drink.

She glanced over at me and smiled. I nodded back. Although she was heavy, she reminded me of Abigail Burns, the librarian. It was something about her posture and the way her mouth turned. No doubt they were related. Abigail had been part of the community forever.

I used to see Abigail whenever I went to visit my Aunt Daisy because she lived just down the road. With Daisy renting her little house and living in the big house with me, I didn't get over there nearly as much.

I considered asking the woman if she and Abigail were related but decided against it. While she might look a bit like Abigail, she was much heftier. I didn't want to embarrass myself. When Cheri put the drink up, the woman thanked her, gave her a tip, and left, moving quickly and easily in a way that reminded me of Abigail. Perhaps I had been right in the first place. I needed to stop judging people by their size.

"So?" Cheri asked.

"You know, the thing was, he mentioned her having a relative named Andy come by. The odd thing is a woman named Elle Mabry came over to talk to me because she knew Gram. Her son Evan has disappeared. And guess what? Evan is married to a guy named Andy," I said. "Do you think it could be the same person?"

That was as far as I could go without confessing my psychic abilities, which I did not want to do in Cheri's coffee house.

"You do know my mother always heard people saw your Gram for psychic readings?" Cheri asked, leaning over the counter like she was going to climb over it.

"I did not know that," I said. "And you didn't say anything why?"

"You were always so weird about psychic stuff. Remember you wouldn't even ever go to movies if they had a psychic type person in them or you thought they might because you thought psychic ability was so ridiculous. I know you got it from your mother and all, but it seemed way over the top, particularly when folks always talked about psychic stuff with your grandmother," Cheri said. Her look dared me to challenge her on that.

Cheri may be about an inch shorter than I am with a rounded Venus de Milo figure, but she can also be pretty tough. I wouldn't want to take her on if she got mad at me.

"My mom *was* weird about it. I didn't want to have to explain to her what I'd been doing," I said. That was certainly the truth. Plus, I didn't want her hearing about me and my psychic abilities.

Cheri nodded and smiled. "So, I bet this Elle wanted to know if you were psychic, too."

"Actually, she was hoping I could help her using psychic abilities. I guess she'd gone to Gram before and Gram had helped her."

"So? Was your Gram psychic?" Cheri started bouncing again.

"I guess," I said. I hoped Cheri wouldn't ask the next obvious question. "And if she was, at least now maybe I have an idea about the Andy that Layla might have had over. He's supposed to be a distant relative. Do you know the Mabrys at all? Or Layla?"

Cheri shook her head. "It's a small town, but I don't know everyone. Layla preferred her own home brewed herbal tea to anything we make here. From what I've heard, that's probably a good thing because no one liked her, but you knew that."

Did I ever.

"Think you can find out anything about the Mabrys or Evan's husband, Andy?" I asked.

"What can you tell me about Andy?" Cheri asked.

"I know he works as a sous chef. Evan was in IT, so I bet he made the majority of the money. Also, Andy's last name is Willard."

Cheri nodded, biting her lip. "And you said that Layla might be related to him?"

"That's what Harry suggested, but I think he meant not a close relative."

"You know that property off Cliff Street?" Cheri asked.

I gave her a long look. Cliff was one of the streets that angled off of the main streets through the tiny area that was known as downtown Seales. While there were plenty of houses, most of them built around the turn of the century, once you passed the railroad tracks that ran through town, angling down towards Versailles and Lawrenceburg, there wasn't much out there.

Driving out that way meant you saw plenty of cows and a few horses. I think someone might even have had hogs, but I couldn't swear to it. There was also plenty of corn growing out there and at one time they grew tobacco, but most of that was gone.

Cheri sighed. "It's about a mile down the road, just before the road splits to go towards the river?"

I knew the junction she meant. There was a huge farm on the left side. At the split was a series of three small homes, all brick and no more than eight hundred square feet. They were tiny places, probably built as starter homes after the war.

The land on the other side, before the split, had an old fence that was falling apart, a bit of rock work along the gully, and not much else. It was overgrown and an old creosote black gambrel-roofed barn was falling to pieces. I couldn't ever remember someone living there, not that it was a road we took much. There wasn't much out there unless you lived there.

"I think so," I said.

"I think at one time it belonged to the Willard family. My mom knew about it when she was a kid. Guess the Willards who farmed died off and then no one took care of it. It's been for sale as long as I can remember."

I nodded. I remembered that at one time there'd been a sign. That was long gone, probably blown away by a windstorm or stolen on a high school dare, though it wasn't much of a dare, not nowadays.

"I'll have to ask her," Cheri said. "See if there was other family that just didn't want to farm or something?"

"That'd be great. It would be interesting to see if Andy did have a connection to Layla."

"Maybe he wanted to poison his husband and was looking into a way of doing it," Cheri said. "And then he got rid of Layla because she knew too much?"

"Except Evan isn't dead. He's just missing."

Cheri shrugged. "Maybe it takes time for the poison to get out of his bloodstream and so he'll turn up later?"

Now that was a thought. It didn't seem likely because too much could go wrong, but it wasn't impossible.

"Uh, oh." Cheri smiled at me, suddenly a Cheshire cat, all teeth and knowing eyes.

I looked around. Byron Cabot had just come in. He looked more relaxed, although he seemed a bit embarrassed to see me there.

Chapter 14

I smiled at Byron, hoping to put him at ease. The soft music that was playing in the background, some sort of elevator version of Madonna—and no, those two things do not go together—seemed to put him a little more at ease. He gave his order and got it, a plain coffee, before walking over to me.

"I'm sorry about what happened at the office," he said.

"Nothing happened," I said. What can I say? Sometimes I lie.

"It did," Byron insisted. "Sandra and I went out for a while, but it's never worked. Her family doesn't approve of my job, and she's not willing to buck them. I think she's afraid that they'll cut her out of the will. She says she'd like to leave, but a few years back, I offered. She declined."

"Wow," I said. "It sounded like she had something to tell you, though."

"She's always got something to tell me," Byron said. "Mostly it happens if it looks like I'm getting involved with someone. I had hoped that taking our relationship a bit slow would keep it under her radar and by the time she attempted to get back into my life, we'd be together. I figured I'd know you well enough that I could tell you about her and you wouldn't write me off as some guy with a crazy ex you didn't want to get involved with, but here I am. A guy with an ex who doesn't want to let go."

"Seales is a small town," I said. "I'm not exactly unknown, either to people who knew me when I grew up here or else from when Marty died. It'd be obvious if she heard something." I felt vaguely uncomfortable that Sandra might only be seeing me because she wanted to know the woman Byron was dating. I hoped that I'd helped her enough that that was a secondary consideration for her now.

Byron nodded. "I figured keeping things on a friend level might have worked. I probably should have left town, but I'm attached to Seales. I like it here, like the people, mostly, and like the pace. It's not far from my family up in Indianapolis. I can go into a city if I want—heck I have my choice of city flavor and size, really—and I have a good job in a place where I can still be respected. We're small enough that I don't have the same level of departmental politics. Mostly I don't have to worry about the other police officers acting like jerks and giving us all a bad a name in town."

I could understand that. Even Vancouver and Portland had had their share of police problems.

"It's just Sandra. She thinks that because she wants me on her terms, I should just bow down and take what I can get. At one time, I might have felt that I had to." Byron finally finished.

"But you don't anymore?" I asked.

Byron shook his head. My heart fluttered because that's what I wanted to hear. I mean I wanted to hear more about how he'd changed after meeting me or something romantic like that, but this was far more practical. I loved that he seemed just a little bit embarrassed but in a nice way.

"I probably should have said something sooner," he said quietly. "She couldn't have picked a worse time, either, given that I've had to distance myself from you a little bit."

I wondered if Sandra had known that he'd be there. Of course, there was no way she could have unless she'd been the one to break in. I thought back to the person who had broken into the office, but they hadn't moved in the same way she moved. I was pretty sure they were taller, too. Besides, they'd been dressed in dark clothing that appeared to be a hoodie, keeping me from seeing their hair, and I just couldn't see Sandra even owning a hoodie. Not at all her style.

"I'm okay moving on now that I know," I said, "assuming that you still want to after this case gets cleared up."

Byron nodded. "It's too bad I'm off it. It's a huge case. I don't think we've found anyone who actually liked Layla. I'm not sure if she could talk that she'd say she liked herself all that much either."

I considered telling him what I knew about the name Andy. Instead I changed the subject.

"I heard there's a missing persons, too," I said.

Byron looked confused.

"Evan Mabry?"

"Oh. That case. Technically, that's county so it's their baby. Evan didn't live in the city limits. Not that his mother cares. She's been hounding us about it, saying the county police aren't doing their jobs, and she wants us to look into it. Problem is, we don't have any jurisdiction because there's nothing to suggest he disappeared from anywhere but his home. He could have disappeared in Lexington, I guess, but that's even further out of my jurisdiction."

"I didn't know that," I said. I filed all that away. "It must be real hard for her."

"I can't imagine having a child go missing," Byron said. There it was, that kindness that drew me to him. Well, that and he was pretty nice looking.

"I can't either," I said. "I'd probably be grasping at straws as well." Particularly if they were straws my missing child might have liked and held. With them, I might have gotten clues. Naturally, I'd do my own investigation. How much was Elle doing?

"He might be an adult, but it is damned strange. We've made some inquiries, and the county knows that she's been trying to get us to take over, so they've shared a few things. They can't find anything out of place. The only thing at all out of the ordinary was that in the last few months he was writing large checks to a company that's some sort of shell company. They're still digging into the parent company and owners, but it's slow going."

"Do they think that had anything to do with his disappearance?" I asked.

"It seems suspicious," Byron said. "But we don't know. It's possible he was getting taken by a scam that was completely separate from his disappearance. I mean, the county's investigating the company—it's all they have, really—but there's no guarantee the answers will be of any help."

I noticed that Byron seemed to think that Evan was missing and alive. I had worried he'd think he was dead. The twenty-four hour thing and all, but perhaps that was only for children?

"He was married to Andy Willard, wasn't he?" I asked.

Byron nodded. "Nice guy. Talked to him when he came in once with Elle, before he realized we weren't just another office of the county sheriff's."

"I heard his family had property off of Cliff Street." I wondered what Byron would do with that.

"Not your place to go searching for a missing person," Byron said, his voice becoming more authoritarian.

"Not looking. Just making conversation. It came up in some other gossip. I thought it was interesting. I hadn't heard who owned that old barn before. It's been vacant forever."

And, I thought, probably a great place to hide a body, especially if you were Andy or if you were someone trying to make it look like Andy had killed Evan.

I got a tingle down my back. There was that old falling-down barn. If you wanted to hide someone there, wouldn't a falling-down barn be a good place to do it? It wasn't like Cliff Street out that far was all that busy. If you set up a small room inside, it would be easy enough to hold someone.

Byron and I talked a bit more. I watched him leave and then dumped my coffee with only a wave at Cheri. I was going to head out to the Willard property while I was thinking about it.

Chapter 15

I found a pull out to park in on Cliff Street, barely in view of the little houses up ahead. The houses were even more forlorn than I remembered, the white siding looking gray, and, in a few places, starting to fall off. Moss grew on the roof of the one closest and there were bushes that were easily taller than I was growing up along the corner. I wondered if you could even see out of the windows.

I smelled dirt and the faintest scent of gasoline. I had no idea where that came from. I didn't see any stains on the blacktop or on the gravel of the pullout. The creosote split rail fence was falling in, and most of the rail was no longer black but a dull gray. As I stepped towards the property, I noticed that at one time there had been stone fencing made free-hand of local limestone. It was standing up better than the split rail but only just, time and climate wearing it down into the ground rather than causing it to fall.

The same sort of thing was going on out at Gram's, too. The property along the main road was lined with limestone fencing, but you could see places where it wasn't very high, though at one time it had been. Every time they dug a ditch along the side of the road, the stone sank a little deeper. We added dirt to the area, pushing the stone deeper into the earth. In some distant future, archaeologists would wonder about the way the limestone fences were laid out.

I started walking across the field. I had on nice khaki trousers and they were heavily made. Fortunately, it was early enough in the spring that the grasses were only up to the middle of my calf and not all the way up to my knees. I kept my eyes on the ground, not wanting to twist my ankle in a hole or something.

The clouds were coming in bringing a slight breeze, which brought the soft rustle of grasses. It was chillier today than yesterday. We were definitely in for some rain, probably sooner rather than later. This wasn't good for me in terms of searching out in a field, but hopefully the barn had enough roof that if rain did start before I finished, I could take shelter there.

I didn't even let myself think what I would do if there was someone being held out there. I had my cell phone. I paused to check that I had service and I did. Thank heavens for flatter lands so that you could be out in the country and still have service. Of course, if you got too far out, you might not, but this close to town, even in a small town, you could generally get a couple of bars.

The barn seemed further away than it had when I drove by. It was even more run-down than I remembered, the frame listing ever so slightly to the left. From here, I noted that boards were missing and the ones that were there were only dark and lighter gray with no black to be seen. The gambrel roofline was even starting to fall in a bit, leaving holes here and there.

I listened for any other cars, but there was no one going down the street. I felt that was both good and bad. Good in that no one was there to question my right to be there. Bad in that I was pretty much alone.

Turning back was tempting, but when I looked around, I realized I was at least halfway to the barn. I kept on walking.

The land was lumpy and bumpy and there were plenty of sticks, some wood, and even stray garbage that had been left in the field at one time or another. I even came across an old red and black wool blanket that had been spread out on the ground. It was filled with holes and partially eaten. I avoided stepping on it, not sure what was under the thing, and kept on going.

A few early spring wildflowers were near to blooming. In a month they would brighten the field with their color.

The closer I got to the barn, the larger and more decrepit it looked. It wasn't just partially falling down, half the roof was gone, fallen in. The boards were on the ground, broken and worn. Near the ground, many of the long side boards were missing.

The barn had only one door, the other was laying on the ground in front of the building. I got closer, wondering if it was a good idea to go inside. I didn't have a flashlight and the day was just dark enough that the gray boards made it hard to make out what was going on in the shadows.

The weeds and grass continued a few feet inside the doors, though the land was smoother there. Heavy equipment would have pressed the earth flatter closer to the barn. I wondered what the barn was used for. It looked like it might have been a tobacco barn rather than cows, though I thought I remembered cows from when I was a kid.

Inside, along the wall that still had a roof, or part of one, there were some support posts. A few interior walls, about waist high, remained standing, though boards laid over on the side from a couple of them.

Looking under the roof, I could see where some of the supports were still standing but others had been pushed over when the roof fell in. I walked carefully inside, not liking the way the roof hung but not willing to turn back now that I was there.

I looked down at the floor but didn't see any trap doors or depressions that might catch an ankle. Low, scraggly weeds covered the ground even further into the barn. Nothing looked like a room within a building.

Stubbornly, I kept on. I had had a feeling there was something there. A rake was lying across the way. The tines gleamed. I went to step around it and then thought better of it. A rake laying there should be rusted and old. Heck, the ones at our barn tended to rust and they were in a far better place than this was.

I touched the rake near the bottom with only my palm, avoiding getting fingerprints on it.

Nausea rose. Terror. Something had happened. Something I couldn't come back from. I pulled my hand away because if I didn't, I was going to be sick. I didn't know what had happened, but whoever had left the rake had done something, something that made them sick to think about.

Andy's family owned the land. He and Evan could have been out there. What if something had happened to Evan? Maybe the two of the fought?

It didn't feel right, but I stood up and looked around, looked for a reason someone would bring a rake to this old barn. The weeds covered nearly everything, still scraggly and unkempt. Except in one corner. That corner was dirt, freshly raked.

The ground had been turned, raked and perhaps dug up. Nothing had been digging at it since, so if it was a body, it was buried deep enough not to attract scavengers.

I bit my lip.

I turned around, taking stock of the barn from this end. Something gleamed in the dirt. I went over to it.

I found an earring. I allowed myself to open to see what impressions I could get. Immediately, Layla Wiltshire came to mind. I knew beyond a doubt this was her earring. They'd been a gift and had given her joy until they didn't. Something had happened, but it was vague. The joy was there and then a sort of distaste for the joy.

I got an impression of the earrings being put on for a date. For a meeting with the thought that they'd bring luck. Hands touched these for luck, not always Layla's hands, but I didn't know who else touched them, only that someone else did.

Someone related. Maybe Andy? Maybe Andy's mother or sister? It felt like someone close to him.

Something dripped upon my head.

I opened my eyes, wiping the earring on my shirt. The rain had started.

Thunder cracked and the wind picked up, making the whole building shake. A board hanging down from the roof broke off even with that small wind. It fell towards me. I started to run towards the far entrance, hoping I'd get to the edge before anything else collapsed.

Chapter 16

The loose boards on the roof banged and slammed against each other in the wind. Another piece fell as I broke into a run. When I got to the main entrance and felt the rain whipping around, I looked back. The roof itself hadn't collapsed, just a few more boards had fallen. Those that were merely loose were slowly wearing their way through whatever fasteners held them.

I looked out at the thick, heavy rain drops. I pulled my head back in, staying by the door, keeping an eye on the roof. I hoped that this wouldn't be one of the rare storms that went on for hours. Normally in Seales, it rains hard for a little while and then tapers off or stops altogether for the day. I didn't know which this would be, but I hoped it would stop soon.

Even if it was just tapering, I could run for the car, hopefully not hurting myself in the process.

The day was dark now, the clouds low. I saw a gray sedan cruising down the road, going slowly, wheels pitching up water where there was a low spot in the road. I hoped my car was safe in the pull out. Despite the clouds, I hadn't noticed the grade of the land when I'd parked.

I listened to the drum and splatter of the water and tried to organize my thoughts. I knew that Layla had been here and probably Andy, though I didn't know that latter for certain. Someone had done something terrible, leaving freshly turned earth in the corner.

Looking at my phone, I tried to decide how mad Byron would be if I reported the loosened earth. No matter how mad he was, I had to report it. Who knows what could be buried in that corner?

I was hoping it was nothing. I couldn't discount the fact that it might be Evan Mabry down there. The worse part was, if it was Evan, I had been the one to find him. Again. Fingers were likely to continue pointing at me.

As I placed the call, I kept my eyes on the roof. I couldn't help but worry that it was all going to come tumbling down while I stood there. No matter that it had lasted how many storms over the years, the way my luck was, it would happen when I was there.

When Byron answered, I told him where I was and what I had found.

I heard a sigh that could have meant many things. He was on his way. I was ordered to stay in the barn. I figured if the building fell in, waiting in my car would be good enough.

Waiting was hard. I'm used to wet having lived out just outside Portland, Oregon, where I'd studied acupuncture and then set up my first practice. Kentucky rain is a different sort of wet. There's a humidity in the air and the rain drops are larger. The good news was that by the time I saw Byron's squad car turning into the pullout near mine, the rain had mostly stopped.

I stuck my hands under my arms, waiting. My shirt was damp but not soaked. I remained by the door. Drops fell from the sides of my hair. The barn had been shelter but not much of one.

Byron walked through the field more quickly than I had, picking his way carefully while still hurrying. It didn't seem like it took him nearly as long to get there as it had taken me. Longer legs, maybe? Maybe I'd been slow because I'd felt guilty about potentially trespassing?

"Did I or did I not tell you to not go and investigate?" Byron asked.

"You said not to. But this bothered me. I really

didn't expect to find anything but an old barn," I said.

Byron nodded, following me back through the barn. The roof boards were still clacking. A particularly large gust of wind had a piece of a board falling towards the floor behind us.

"I can't believe you spent the entire storm in here," he said. "You could have been killed."

"I was by the door and I watched the roof. I could have gotten out if something had happened."

Byron didn't dignify that with an answer, just shaking his head. I knew it was probably foolish, but how could you tell how foolish until you got out there?

I saw him notice the rake which was still lying on the ground.

Then in the back corner I saw him squat down and look around the area, noting what looked turned up and what didn't.

"Could be anything buried in there," Byron said.

I frowned, wishing for something else.

Byron got up and looked around. I saw him walk towards an area near where the roof had fallen and then squat.

He pulled out a cell phone and made a call.

I stepped over by him. I looked at the dark spot he was kneeling by and knew in my gut that he'd found blood. Considering the angle of the boards, I wondered if someone had been standing there and was hit and killed or if something else had happened.

I remembered the sensations that came from the rake. Could it have been accident? That didn't feel quite right.

"Do you think the roof fell and hit someone and someone else tried to cover it up?" I asked.

Byron shrugged. "Not impossible. Someone worried about liability leaving this place up. It's a hazard. Now that we're here, I suspect someone will be citing the Willards even if it's not a crime scene. Imagine if there were kids out here?"

That would be a disaster I didn't want to contemplate.

We waited while another officer drove up. I was pleased to see it wasn't Gil Daffney. Instead it was a middle-aged man I hadn't met before. I watched him walk across the field. He was just a little chubby around the middle but his legs were slender. His hair was either very short or he was bald.

Once he reached us, I noted that he was bald, his face lined from the weather, already sporting a hint of a tan. His eyes were blue.

"Officer Drake Springer," Byron said, introducing me to him.

Drake nodded at me. He had some sort of

equipment and headed over to the corner of the building. He scanned the ground, getting an image of what was there. From the shadows, I would say there was definitely something under there, but I couldn't say what.

Drake and Byron nodded at each other.

Byron made another call while Drake headed back to the car. When he returned, he had shovels. The two men began digging. It wasn't long before they hit blue fabric. While Drake dug around the area, Byron knelt and started brushing away dirt to see what was in the fabric.

As he did so, a hand fell to the side, flesh still clinging to it, though barely. Whoever this was, it wasn't Evan unless he'd been dead a lot longer than I was given to believe.

Chapter 17

Forensics was called, and I was hustled out of the way. Byron took me by the arm and told me I had to wait in the car.

We walked quickly across the field, under clouds that were beginning to clear, the dark gray giving way to fluffy white interspaced with blue sky. The wind had died down, but there was enough of a breeze to ruffle my hair now and then. The field smelled cleaner than it had, the rain carrying away the smells of dead foliage and slight rot, at least for the moment.

"Would it be okay if I went home?" I asked. I had no desire to sit in my little Honda Fit for hours.

"So long as you keep me informed where you are," Byron said.

"What about the blood? It seemed fresher than the body?" I asked.

"I can't comment on that or speculate," Byron said, though I knew he was wondering the same thing. I couldn't help but think the body and the fresher-looking blood was tied to Layla and Evan. Maybe Layla had been out there and found the body?

I mulled possibilities over on the drive home. It was strange to me that I now thought of Gram's as home. It had been Gram's for forever. I pulled into the drive and continued around to the garage. The garage had been built long after the house. The original garage, of course, had been the carriage house, which had held carriages for horses to pull. While Gram could have added an attached garage, she'd never driven herself, so having one around behind the old carriage house suited her just fine.

Not that the garage had been newly done or anything. I think the building was as old as I was.

I hadn't cared because when I lived in the carriage house, it was an easy walk.

Daisy was working at a laptop on the kitchen table when I came in. She looked up and smiled at me. "How was your day?"

"Okay," I said. I sat down, wondering if I should tell her about what had happened. Instead I noted the computer and changed the subject.

"You know, we ought to set you up with a real office."

Daisy waved me off. "I'm fine here."

"There are tons of rooms here. We could even break up the old playroom for an office if you didn't find a room you liked."

There was a huge room on the second floor on the wing that jutted into the backyard. We kids had often played in it when the weather was too nasty to be outside. It hadn't been used in years and other than cleaning it from time to time, the doors were rarely opened. We could easily subdivide that into several bedrooms and offices and still have a large bonus room if we wanted such a thing up there.

Daisy just gave me a smile and a nod. "I really like being part of things. I think that's one thing I like about being here. Morgan or Win are always cleaning or straightening or making notes about shopping. I feel like I'm part of something and not just sitting around alone, on my own.

I knew what she meant. There was something nice about the activity around us.

Daisy closed her laptop and leaned forward, "So, have you learned anything about Layla's murder?"

I shook my head. "Just that a lot of people didn't like her."

"I asked around, you know, from the church

ladies this morning." Daisy was fairly active in the Lutheran church. They had a women's Bible study in the morning on Friday. Daisy hadn't ever gone before Marty was killed, but Pastor Frances had been so kind to her. I was really beginning to think there was something going on there. Pastor Francis was nice. The only thing that bothered me about the potential relationship was that it might mean Daisy would move out of the house.

"And?" I asked, also leaning forward across the table. It was small enough that I could smell the faint traces of lilac soap that Daisy had used that morning.

"Well," Daisy began, leaning back and folding her hands, "Pastor didn't know her but one of his neighbors did. She was talking about it last night."

I waited while Daisy took a breath, her fair skin and graying hair looking frail in the light. I wondered when she had gotten old. Is that what losing a child did to someone?

"She thought Layla had gotten what she deserved. Apparently, Layla was often up in people's business, not just criticizing their business, like she did with yours, but criticizing the way they lived. She was very environmentally oriented and very animal rights oriented, but she liked to talk rather than do, you know?"

I nodded, thinking about other things I had heard. Rather than going out and starting a program to help horses, she'd have complained about the way they were treated at one of the stables, even if the complaint was unfair. She'd done the same with my business. She hadn't learned about it at all, merely said that I didn't know what I was doing. She was confident that she knew more than anyone else but had no desire to change anything.

"Anyway, I guess Layla didn't like the fact that this woman wore fake fur, thinking it was real. Layla screamed at her in the parking lot one winter. Even after learning the coat was fake, whenever this woman ran into Layla, she'd get a lecture about wearing fur. That was only one story. Nancy also had her own story."

Nancy was a friend of Daisy's. I remembered her from the funeral, a short woman with red hair too bright for her age but a kind face. She'd done a lot to help out after Marty had died. I know my mom had appreciated having someone else who could spend time with Daisy when she'd needed to come home from time to time.

Nancy had helped organize Daisy's move and helped her clean out the house and sort stuff she wanted to keep and what could go. I think she was probably a bigger practical helper than Pastor Francis.

"Nancy said that Danielle at Hoskins farms had a run in with Layla just a few days before she died. For about a month, Layla had been claiming that Hoskins mistreated their horses. She'd often had signs around outside the farm, just on the public right of way near the road, saying racing should be abolished—you know they have some winners there and breed for racing?—anyway, I guess she saw one of the horses being set up for stud and had a fit, thinking they were mistreating it."

I remembered learning about the ways in which they protected the horses who were standing stud. No owner wanted an angry mare biting or kicking their prized stud. No owner of a prized mare wanted her damaged by a stud, so the females wore protective coats. The males had protection against being kicked. It was certainly a production. I found it amazing that horses were ever bred at all considering they were as choreographed as any love scene in Hollywood.

"Danielle wasn't even part of the breeding that day. She happened to be mucking out the stables where Layla could see her and recognized her. She started yelling. Danielle was the one who had to ask her to leave. When Layla refused and kept up the yelling even after the horse was led away, Danielle had to call the police to have her removed. Since then, Layla has been, as Nancy said, practically lying in wait to yell at Danielle about working at a stable that abuses its horses."

It sounded like all the other stuff. Enough to

make people angry and frustrated but never physically harmful. Just mental stuff. It had to get to someone.

"I've heard about the people who want to stop horse racing," I said. It hadn't been such a big deal in the west. While there were racetracks out there, racing wasn't life the way it felt here. I'd seen protestors outside Keeneland last fall when I'd been running into Lexington for something on a race day.

"I have, too. I guess I do feel for the horses that have died, but I just can't think how not racing them helps," Daisy said. "I think some of those horses live better than most people I know. Even your grandfather's horses lived better than some people. I mean, even our boarders, with Jaci, basically have their own staff!"

I laughed. I didn't think our horse boarders were that pampered. They were well cared for and the tiny staff was important because Gram certainly wasn't running the barn. Neither was I, when it came to that. In fact, sometimes I wondered why I had boarders at all. It had brought in a bit of money for Gram. It had allowed her to make sure Marty had a place to keep her horse. It had also meant that she'd not had to make a decision to take down the barn that my grandfather had had built for his horses.

At some point I was going to have to decide if that was important to me, too.

"It seemed like Layla pissed a lot of people off," I said. "But nothing seems like it's enough to kill her, you know?"

"It just takes one person pushed too far," Daisy said. "I mean, think about Marty. Her murder makes no sense at all because you didn't even care about the inheritance. It just took one person twisting that information in his mind and she was dead."

"Are you saying that whoever killed Layla didn't have all the facts?"

"Maybe she threatened to say something to someone?" Daisy asked.

Or perhaps she knew something about someone that needed to be said. I thought of the blood in the barn. There was the earring as well.

I heard the door swing open behind me. I looked up. Morgan came in carrying bags of groceries. It's amazing how much he purchases every three or four days, but somehow Win makes use of it all and we eat well. The bill isn't all that high considering how much it appears he buys. I'm often surprised that the grocery store has any food left after he goes shopping.

I got up to help him carry stuff in.

"Don't you worry none, Miss Ash," Morgan said quietly. "I got this."

"No problem," I said.

"I know you've had a long day. Heard about what you found in the barn off Cliff Road. Guess the police are looking at Andy Willard for that seeing he's the only family around. Place is technically his. They are particularly interested because he's married to Evan Mabry, who's gone missing."

"Wasn't Elle just here the other day?" Daisy asked.

I nodded and told her what Elle wanted.

"Did you see anything?" Daisy asked.

"Nothing that seemed helpful. All I got was money problems and someone pushing for more money. I think it was Evan holding the pen, but I could be wrong." I hated this.

Morgan just nodded. "Miz Beauvoir always said you could only say what you saw and not make judgments. Someone else might take your feeling and make more sense out of it than you because they know more."

Which was an interesting perspective. I wish Gram was there to guide me. She'd taught me a lot about protecting myself, how not to pick up random information, how to make sure I picked up information when I wanted, but nothing about talking to people about what I saw. I wished that I could go back and ask her.

Chapter 18

I didn't have any patients that Saturday, for which I was glad. I was distracted by the murder, by what I had learned about Byron, and by what I had found out at the barn. Byron hadn't told me anything about what they had found, which was driving me nuts.

On the one hand, I understood that I was likely still a possible suspect, but on the other hand, I wanted to know everything to be sure I was getting marked off that suspect list. There seemed like there were all these loose ends. Once again, I resolved that I was not ever going to be a detective. Of course, then I wouldn't be suspect every time a dead body turned up, either.

When Marty had died, Claire Wilcox had followed me around. At least there was no one tailing me, even Gil Daffney, who had seemed to believe I was a likely suspect in Layla's murder.

It was important to focus on the good.

At least I was in good company as a suspect. Everyone else in my little commercial complex was being questioned as well. While we were probably all suspects, I think that there was also the possibility that at least one of us was a victim.

After being formally questioned, I knew that Layla had been killed in the middle of the night.

I had been home, asleep, as most people would be at that time. It was hard to have an alibi when you're asleep. At least that would be true of most everyone else. I was also glad that I was still living in the big house where there were more people around. The house might be too big for someone to hear me sneak out, but at least it made it that much harder to sneak around.

Cheri called me midmorning. I had finished some toast and a few rashers of bacon. I was having a large cup of coffee and letting the fumes wake me. Win was rinsing the pans out in the sink, the running water a white noise behind me, along with the fan over the stove.

Daisy had gone upstairs already, having finished her breakfast a bit earlier, so I was alone, watching the slight breeze move the newly green leaves on the bushes out back.

"What's up?" I asked.

"I heard that you found a body in the old Willard barn, and I know you weren't the one who told me," Cheri said.

"I found disturbed earth so I called the police. They were the ones who actually found the body. I was told to leave so I didn't have anything to say."

"I can't believe you went out there. I would have been far too scared and with that weather yesterday, the way that barn leans and the roof falling in like that, you could have been buried alive and then what would we have done?"

"I'm fine." I hoped Cheri wasn't going to go on about this.

"Well, you know that they're questioning Andy Willard about all this and it does not look good considering that his husband, Evan, has gone missing. I heard that Evan's mother is all up in arms about him going missing and I have also heard rumors that you read something for her and that you are psychic like your grandmother. This is also something I feel I should have heard from you."

"I don't know who's saying I'm psychic," I said. "I'm not really. Sometimes I pick up things when I touch them, but I'm not like able to do it at will. I let Elle come in and talk to me, that's all."

I got a sound that suggested Cheri wasn't at all pleased with the answer. I was definitely going to have to come up with a better one the next time we talked. I had a feeling she'd let that go this time but not for long.

"I never really talked about it because no one believed me when I said things," I added lamely. "Besides, my mother hated the idea I might know things. It really wasn't to be discussed in our house."

I got a better grunt this time as Cheri were more willing to be placated, although she still wasn't pleased.

"So? What do you know about Evan Mabry and Elle? I know you were talking to me about them earlier."

"Just what Elle told me, which was that he was missing. I worry that Andy did something, not because of any psychic information I have, but because it's sort of the obvious question, isn't it?" I said.

"It is, except I heard that the body in the barn was too far gone to be Evan unless Andy had done something to it to make it decompose faster," Cheri said.

I always wondered how she heard so much. Even in the coffee shop, people didn't gossip that much. Maybe she had her own psychic abilities.

"Do you know if it was a man or a woman?" I asked. I wasn't even sure about that.

"Oh, it's a man, all right," Cheri said. "I heard that much."

"You know more than I do."

"For once."

"It's not like I keep things from you."

"You had that talk with Detective Cabot right there in the coffee shop and hardly told me anything. Then you had to be begged to tell me what you learned from Harry when I was the one who wanted you to go talk to him."

"It's not like I learned all that much. Hey, something I didn't mention to Byron because it totally slipped my mind. I found an earring out at the barn. Do you know if Layla liked earrings?" I asked.

"Did you leave the earring there?"

"Yes, I just saw it and nudged it to see what it was. That was when I saw the earth was disturbed, and I forgot about it until we were talking."

"See. It's good to confide in someone. You remember things, so you ought to do it more often."

"I expect that having a body out there means that forensics will have found the earring, too. It wasn't buried or anything. It was just kind of lying there. Like this new rake. Why a rake? You'd think if you needed new tools to bury someone, you'd use a shovel."

"Maybe they took the shovel but someone scared them off before they got the rake." Cheri said.

“Easy enough to carry both.” Unless, of course, one had a body with them because they’d already taken the shovel and were just smoothing the earth. Maybe Layla had found them and then they’d murdered her, too. Could that be the way it went down?

“Maybe they brought other tools. A pick or something like that? Or maybe they had to take away clothing and stuff,” Cheri said. She wasn’t wrong. All of those were possibilities.

“I’m actually kind of glad that I haven’t heard much from the police,” I said. “It seems like I’m not under quite as much suspicion as I was when Marty died.”

“Well, it’s not like you’re the main suspect this time. What Layla said about you seems to be par for the course, at least so far as I’ve heard, and I’ve been asking. If someone knows her or knows of her, they know of someone she bad-mouthed. And she bad-mouthed just as many businesses. I heard about the pet store, the grocery store, that little bakery down on Elm.”

“What did she say about the bakery?” That was a new one. The pet store was too, but I’d expected that, given Layla’s hang-ups about animals.

“Just that they used substandard recipes. I think she claimed to have gotten food poisoning there once, but that was from Winnie Tragger and she’s not the most reliable of sources. Two other people mentioned Layla telling folks not to go to the bakery, which would certainly piss me off. I guess Geri Paulson who runs the place is having a hard time staying afloat. She's just too far off the beaten path and with the new grocery store up there selling so many different baked goods, she's lost some of her regulars. She wants to move someplace where there are more people thinking about food. Even around the corner onto Main would work for her, although she's hoping for something over by you."

"I think that at this point it might be easier to think about who isn't mad at Layla. Maybe they're hiding something?" I said, only half joking.

Geri was interesting though. If she wanted a place out by me, a dead body, namely the body of her enemy being found out there and putting us under suspicion, might free up a space. I could be seen as the easiest mark as my office was the newest and I had the smallest business. Plus, Layla had recently been very active in bad-mouthing me. Could it be that easy?

"Hey, I have to go. We need to do lunch. Maybe after church tomorrow?" Cheri said.

"Sounds good." I hung up the phone, thoughtfully. The sun was out and it was a nice morning. I just wanted to relax but there were some business items I had to take a look at. Being a majority shareholder of a bourbon company came with responsibilities that I hadn't really foreseen. Now I had to learn the ropes.

Someone banged on the side door. I heard Morgan hurrying to answer it. I waved him off as I walked over to the door. He joined me there.

I opened the door and there was Officer Drake Springer.

"I'm here to take more of a statement about the body you found yesterday and how you came to find it," Drake said. He gave me a long look and then glared up at Morgan as if he didn't like him.

"Come in," I said, trying to be pleasant.

Morgan backed up, but he was moving stiffly.

"Morgan. Fleeced any more old ladies?" Drake snarked.

Morgan drew in a breath, said nothing, just turned and left like a dog who had been beaten.

I turned to glare at Officer Springer, suddenly angry. What had Morgan ever done to him?

Chapter 19

I wished I hadn't been so shocked by the altercation that I could have said something more to Officer Springer. Instead, I remained silent, not sure what to say.

I led Springer to the breakfast nook. Win had already whisked away the dish I had been using, though she'd left my coffee. The table was crumb free. I noticed she, too, had disappeared. Apparently, Springer was known.

I had no desire to let the officer further into the house. In fact, if I had thought of it, I might have talked to him on the porch, had I known how he'd treat Morgan.

As I sat, letting Springer decide if I was going to allow him to sit or not, I asked him about his comment.

"Oh, come on. A guy like that… he only stayed on for your grandmother's money. Look at what it's gotten him. He lives here."

"He works here and part of his compensation is living space," I said. "*I* pay him now, not my grandmother. He has certain duties that he carries out no matter that the will stipulates he has a place to live here so long as he desires. And yes, there was a package for him in the will, but I think when you live with someone for decades, that's natural, don't you?"

Springer made a face and glared at me, not saying anything. Clearly his issue with Morgan had more to do with a general dislike than anything else.

"You came here to ask about what I saw at the barn," I prompted when Springer seemed off his game. Of course, I had to admit, antagonizing him probably wasn't the best way to go. It seemed that no matter what, somehow I found a way to antagonize the police I was working with.

While Byron and I got along, there was more than a little romantic interest, which had its own pitfalls. Even when an officer wasn't trying to link me to a crime, I had to go and pick a fight over something that wasn't related.

Springer nodded and opened a notebook, the old-fashioned kind that flipped over the top and fit in a pocket. He had a pen out and was ready to take notes.

He took me through finding the body, asking if I noticed anything else. I did mention seeing an earring, which was what made me look over at the ground, looking to see if there was a match. Byron hadn't asked specifically about why I looked in the corner, only that I had been there.

I mentioned I had heard that Evan Mabry had gone missing, though I was vague on how I had heard that. I suggested that was what had made me go out to see if he had fallen or something.

"You didn't stop to think that if he had, perhaps Mr. Willard might have considered going out there?" Springer asked. I noticed that he didn't say husband. I wondered what other prejudices might be lurking under the veneer of niceness.

"I don't know Mr. Willard. Even if Evan hadn't been hurt there, he might have left something out of place." I watched Springer's face as he noted that down.

"Layla Wiltshire's murder didn't have anything to do with you going out there?" Springer asked.

"Well, in a roundabout way. I think the conversation about the Willard property came up because of her murder. Isn't she related in some way?"

Springer didn't answer, just made a few more notes.

"Did you notice anything else?"

I shook my head. "I think I only noticed the soft dirt that looked as if someone had been digging and then smoothed it back out. The rain hit just then so I went to the doorway and called Detective Cabot."

Springer nodded. "He called me and we found the body," he said.

"Do you know who it was?" I asked.

Springer shook his head. "Nothing on file as far as fingerprints, and the body isn't recognizable at this point."

He'd paused for just a second as he spoke. I wondered if they had an idea about who it might be. I hadn't heard about anyone else going missing. Cheri hadn't mentioned it either. Given how much she did know, if someone had an idea, they'd have told her.

Two bodies and a missing person. They had to be related. Seales didn't have that much crime. The last time there'd been a little crime wave was when Marty had died. My ex had murdered her and then murdered Clair Wilcox to keep his secret. This situation could be similar. Something had happened, whether a murder or a kidnapping, and the other crimes were related. Knowing which crime came first would help put everything else in order.

Finished speaking to me, Springer got up and left. He gave me a nod as he walked down the few stairs to the squad car, which he'd left in the middle of the drive. If someone else were visiting, they'd have had to wait behind him. Even when unloading the car, Morgan pulled over to the side in case someone else was out and about and wanted to drive past.

I turned to go back in and found Morgan hovering. "I apologize for the incident."

My eyes widened. "What?"

"My apologies for the incident. I had no idea he'd say something here."

"I apologize for you having to put up with that," I said, probably more sharply than I should have.

"Mr. Springer is a man of rather particular sentiments. I don't fit the way things should be, which is apparently much like things were sometime before the Civil War," Morgan said. He got busy rearranging the spices on the counter only to put them back in the same places, or so close to it that I couldn't tell the difference. His hands had the slightest bit of a shake that might have been passed off as old age, but I knew better. He was upset.

"No one here is listening to them," I said.

"Gram left you something for your years of work and because you knew each other. Hell, Morgan, you're practically family. Win's becoming that way, too."

Morgan gave me a smile and a nod. "I could always go to my son's if you decide I'm not needed."

"You know more about Gram's investments than I do. If you weren't helping me out, sorting things, I'd never get it all done."

Another nod. "I should get back to work. I'm mopping floors over in the new wing."

"Great," I said. Those would be his and Win's rooms. Win would probably be heading over to her mom's. She had Saturdays off, though she'd wanted to make bacon and eggs for breakfast.

In theory, they both had Sundays off, but frequently Morgan worked Sundays anyway, at least after church. Sometimes he visited family, but he normally made sure Win was going to be around first. I understood this was habit, particularly in the last couple of years when Gram had been getting a bit frail, but Daisy and I could more than look after ourselves.

I went back to the breakfast table and sat down at it, thinking about all things in life that weren't really fair and all the things I couldn't fix. I wish I could have said more to Morgan about Springer. I wish I had said more to Springer, but as a police officer and one involved with a body I had found, *again*, I hated to antagonize him any more than I already had.

Daisy came downstairs. She was dressed for riding, stretch pants tucked into high boots. Her hair was twisted up and she carried a cap in one hand. Reaching the bottom of the stairs, her color high, she noticed me and hurried over.

"Ash. Oh good. I wanted to talk to you," she said walking into the kitchen. "I called over to the barn to let Jaci know I was going to take Blackjax for a ride, and we got to talking about things."

"What about?" I waited to hear what was so important. I was glad to hear that Daisy was taking out her daughter's horse for a ride. I was so unused to having a horse that I never thought about riding until late at night. I'm not such a good rider that I had any desire to be on our trails after dark when no one was around. Besides, once I was comfortable, it was hard to think about going out.

Of course, was Blackjax actually mine? Gram had technically owned him, but if Marty had lived, I'd have made sure she got to continue as his person. I know that he was missing her attentions.

"Jaci heard a rumor about that body in the barn." Daisy was positively bursting.

I raised an eyebrow waiting.

"Jaci heard that the Hoskins had a guy

working their stables and he just up and disappeared about six months ago. He wasn't local or anything, so they assumed he'd flaked and left town. But people are wondering if that's who's buried there."

Which brought things back to the Hoskins farm. The worker would have had to know Danielle. How well had he known her? And for that matter, had Layla been the one to talk to him and things got out of hand?

Yet another piece of a puzzle that I couldn't quite see the end picture of.

Chapter 20

I spent the afternoon at home thinking about what I learned from Daisy. How did the Hoskins farm play into things? I couldn't concentrate on what I was supposed to be doing. Instead I was searching out information on the Willard and Hoskins farms.

Even then, I didn't learn anything important. The Hoskins had had multiple stakes winners every year for the last decade. That's a good average. They hadn't had any Derby winners, which is huge here, but they were doing well. Stud fees were high.

I had no idea a horse standing stud could be worth the amount some of these horses were. Of course, looking at the bottom line, farms were expensive. There were plenty of horses that ran but didn't win. No matter what, jockeys still had to be paid, grooms still had to be paid, horses still had to eat. The racing business wasn't for me. I'm much more of a make a plan and stick to it kind of person. There were too many things outside my control with racing.

It was tougher going with the Willard farm. It was pretty much gone and had been for a long time. It was only mentioned in a few histories. I found a picture of it in its heyday at the Seales Historical Society Online Album. I also found a picture of Gram's house when it was being built, which I found fascinating.

Something I hadn't noticed was that our bourbon company wasn't that far from the house if you could travel as the crow flies. The river that crossed the edge of the family property and the layout of the roads always made me think it was further.

After my brief bit of family nostalgia, I got back to the Willards. They had mostly just died out. Those who were left hadn't wanted to farm. I didn't get exactly how Layla Wiltshire was related. Chances were, I'd need one of those genealogy sites to learn about the family tree. I wasn't about to set up an account just to research someone else's genealogy. Besides, I wasn't even sure if that was legal.

Just what I needed. Another crime with my name attached to it.

My research left me at loose ends, not wanting to get involved in anything that required my attention. It meant I watched silly movies with Daisy down in the great room until I went to bed.

Cheri was out with a new boyfriend, a guy named Travis. I'd met him once about two weeks ago. From the looks of things, I was thinking that Cheri was getting serious. She certainly deserved someone who treated her well and made her happy. I hoped it all worked out for her.

Sunday morning dawned cloudy and dark. Rain pattered against the windows of my bedroom and it was chillier than it had been in a few weeks. I liked rain but this weather made me think it was going to be harder for techs to search for evidence out at the barn. It wasn't like the roof was going to keep the water out, at least not very well.

I got dressed and headed out to the coffee shop where I'd have a bagel breakfast sandwich, which was pretty incredible, and then sit around and listen to gossip. Maybe Harry O'Reilly would even come in and tell me something interesting.

Once she got up, Cheri would text me about whether we were still on for lunch of if she was too exhausted after last night.

Sunday mornings in the coffee shop weren't as

crowded as I'd have expected, particularly since I was in fairly early. Seales is a church-going community, and I'd heard Daisy leave for service as I was going down the stairs. Morgan and Win also attended services at their own churches in the morning, though when Gram had been ill, Morgan had missed quite often. He'd felt he needed to be around in case she'd needed him.

Thinking about the care he gave her, I got angry with Officer Springer all over again.

I ordered a latte and the breakfast sandwich and settled in to wait. I had a comfortable chair in the corner. Around me the smells of coffee swirled and so did conversations. My corner seat seemed to be in a spot where all conversations were slightly magnified. It was the perfect spot for me to listen in, though I hadn't chosen it for that reason. Mostly, I'd grabbed it because it was one of the few chairs not taken, except for the chintz ones, and I was not making that mistake again.

Two older women, one I recognized as an old friend of Gram's, though her name escaped me, came in. They both wore nice dresses and low-heeled black shoes and nylons. Gram's friend looked over and gave me a two fingered wave. I smiled and waved back, being nice.

The sight of me started them talking about Layla Wiltshire, which I knew they didn't know I could hear.

"Heard she was bad mouthing the acupuncture clinic," the one I didn't know said.

"Can't say that a Beauvoir would do something like that. Remember, she's Bev's granddaughter."

"Of course, could be anyone. Maybe even someone who wants to see that she gets hers, just in case she did set that boy up to take the fall for her killing her cousin."

"Oh hush, you," Gram's friend said, shaking her head. She pointed but did not look in my direction.

This was what I hated about Seales. After having been suspected of a murder once, now everyone was certain I might have had a hand in another. Maybe I'd gotten off with all those murders last time…maybe this…maybe that. Maybe I was a mass murderer with thousands of bodies scattered across the country. I felt my face start to color as I got angrier and angrier.

I forced myself to calm down and listen to the rest of the conversation.

"I got some herbs from Layla once," Gram's friend said as she ordered a medium sized mocha. "Tasted horrible. I swear there were little bugs in the bag she gave me, and she said they would be helpful. I only took them that once, and I can't say they helped at all. Imagine if she was giving everyone those. She could have killed someone."

"I never met her," the stranger said as they moved forward. "I've heard things though. Imagine if she gave something like that to someone and they got sick and died?"

"She was reckless, that's what she was," Gram's friend went on. "She thought she knew more than the doctors and would tell people so."

I took a sip of my latte and smiled. That sounded like Layla, and it was another avenue to consider. I was surprised that Cheri hadn't suggested a revenge killing. Thinking of her, I was beginning to see why she always knew what was going on.

In addition to theories about Layla, which were everything from a secret boyfriend from out of town to a drug ring which she fronted with her legal herb business, I heard about the new high school they were building in Versailles. I heard that people weren't happy about the highway bypass that kept people out of downtown Seales, although others were willing to argue that.

An older man was pontificating on gun rights while two teenage girls giggled about senior prom. It was all very normal.

A couple that looked like a middle-aged husband and wife came in and were whispering together. The hiss of the whisper made me listen in more closely. "I never liked Andy. I think Elle was right on about him. I hate to say it, but I bet Evan is dead," she said.

"We don't know that and you don't need to go upsetting Elle with your theory. She's probably upset enough," the husband said.

"He was always on Evan about money. I heard them arguing that day in the parking lot of the grocery store. I guess Andy wanted to stop over and get some fancy wine in the wine center. Evan said they needed to pare down a few of their little luxuries. Elle doesn't want to believe it, but I know better." The woman was firm.

I decided then and there that I needed to see Andy Willard. I had to find an excuse to talk to him. Maybe I could contact Elle and get an introduction.

The entire coffee shop went quiet as I pondered how to meet Andy. I looked up. A man about my age with dark eyes and dark hair had walked in. He was clean shaven and well dressed in a button-down blue shirt and skinny jeans. He looked uncomfortable at the silence.

I heard someone mumble Andy. So that was the man I wanted to meet. It almost seemed like fate.

Chapter 21

I waited while Andy ordered his coffee. An extra-large frappuccino. Those always took a bit longer to make, so I had some time to think about what to do next. As I started to stand up, I was hit with a blast of the music. Someone had changed the playlist and turned this one up a bit too loud.

A few people in other parts of the coffee shop winced. The woman who thought Andy had murdered Evan was hurrying out with her husband, the bell over the door a counterpoint to the sounds of the music.

I brought my coffee up to my lips and sipped. Andy got his frap and looked around the place, as if he was thinking about staying. I hoped not. I didn't want to talk to him in the coffee shop.

Hadn't I just sat around by myself listening to everyone's conversations?

Other spots might not make it quite so easy to eavesdrop, but I certainly didn't want to be seen talking to Andy. It would fuel the gossips who were certain I was a mass murderer.

Fortunately, Andy breathed out and turned to go. I followed, hoping I wasn't staying too close. Andy kept his head down as he walked out the door.

The parking lot was a narrow thing with angled spaces on the side of the building. There was another pizza delivery place next door. Andy had to walk past it to get to his car. The clouds were low, but the rain was definitely holding off. I expected we'd get a good shower in another hour, but it didn't seem like things were going to be wild while I was outside. I did wish I had a light jacket with me as the slight breeze was chilly.

Andy madc for a nice black BMW. Definitely high style, particularly for a sous chef. Apparently, Evan really did pay for things in the family.

"Andy?" I called after making sure no one else was following us out.

"What?" he demanded, turning.

"I talked to Elle the other day about Evan. I was hoping to fill in some blanks," I said. "I'm Ash Jericho." My full name is Ashley but I go by Ash.

Even my license and official documents just say Ash. Only my birth certificate says otherwise.

"She said she talked to you. Said you thought Evan's disappearance was about money?" Andy seemed a bit hostile. I wasn't sure if this meant he had done something or if there was something else going on.

"That was my impression. Now, I'm not my grandmother by any means, so I could easily have misinterpreted what was going on. Elle didn't think Evan had financial issues, but I figured you'd know better."

Andy frowned at me. "It was an ongoing thing. I like nice things. I work hard, but let's face it, my profession doesn't exactly get me the finest treatment, at least not now. I barely make ends meet. But Evan was doing well and he liked giving me gifts. He was always overspending on me. I didn't need this." Andy gestured to the BMW. "I just wanted a reliable car. I thought maybe a Honda or something. But this…"

He was shaking his head like he didn't understand how Evan had done it.

"Evan makes a good living, but not that good. We had the house which was nice and he was talking about trading up. I'd have loved that. I love decorating and stuff, but I knew with everything else we couldn't afford it."

I watched as Andy made his case for being the

one who didn't want to spend. I had a hard time believing him, but perhaps Evan was that sort of person.

"Do you know of anyone who might have been angry with Evan for not paying bills or something?"

Andy shook his head. "For all that he overspent, he was good about paying the bills. Sometimes he didn't even get stuff for himself, you know? Like he'd drink regular coffee even though he loves fancies just to do a little economizing. I know he never bought himself clothing because he was always buying for me. I was going out and buying him things!"

Like that was a big deal. I wondered if it was to Andy.

"It must be tough right now," I said. "I heard that you were related to Layla Wiltshire."

Andy frowned. "Now that was a horrible thing. Of course, it wasn't like we were close or anything. We saw each other because I had to, you know? My mother made me promise, although she ran off to Florida, saying she liked the weather there, but I think it's because she didn't want to have to see her cousin Layla or be guilted into it. Layla was all over my mom about the way she fed me and my sister, telling her we were going to die young because she didn't breast feed us long enough and didn't feed us organic foods and stuff like that. It was ridiculous to expect that of my mom. She pretty much raised us on her own."

"So, you weren't close to Layla?"

"No one was close to Layla. Just some of us had to put up with her a bit more than others."

"Who would you say wanted to kill her most?" I asked.

Andy rolled his eyes. Then he took a sip of his frap. I sipped my coffee. He leaned against the BMW while I stood straight.

"There are so many," Andy finally said. "I think that she was getting to that woman at the Hoskins farm. Danny, I think. She was livid about what Layla was saying about the horses."

Andy's phone rang and he looked at it. Then he smiled and gave me a two fingered wave. "Got to go," he said. "Duty calls."

He slipped away from me around the front of his car and started to get in. I moved back, not sure what to do. I hadn't gotten the information I wanted. Not that I knew for certain that Andy knew anything. It's just that I had a feeling he knew more than he was telling me.

I walked over to my car just a few spaces down. I got in, still thinking. I sipped at my coffee, piecing things together in my mind. It really seemed like I needed to go talk to Danielle. If nothing else, she could probably tell me about that missing groom. I didn't even have a name for him.

Chapter 22

The Hoskins farm was a fairly large horse farm. They were just west of the city, which was about as far from Gram's place as it was possible to be and still be in Seales. The Hoskins had raised horses in Seales for forever, but it was within my memory when they'd begun expanding their operations. When I was five or six, they had purchased one of the big farms right next to them. It had been a huge deal and my five-year-old self remembered it as being the only thing people talked about for weeks.

Like so many farms, their front property was lined in limestone fencing that had darkened nearly to black. A deep ditch ran between the rock and the road. Just beyond the rock fencing were lines of tulip poplars and pin oaks.

The drive was plain gravel and had a big turnout area. I went past the main house entrance and to the next one, a smaller entrance that didn't have any gates, just a long gravel drive. A few car lengths in, the black split rail fence began, cordoning off various fields for different horses.

Their barn was beige and brown stone rising about halfway up the walls and then a pale beige color siding. The roofline was dark brown. The doors were a dark chocolate colored wood, and the barn was arranged in a u-shape.

I parked in the gravel lot next to a newer black pickup. There were other trucks in the lot across from me, most of them older. I got out and listened.

I heard a few wickers, and I peered through the line of trees that blocked the closest pasture from the line of sight of the parking area. Two horses were out there grazing. A third was rolling around on its back, enjoying the day despite the cool air.

I turned to walk up to the barn. A young woman dressed in heavy khakis stained with grass and a long-sleeved t-shirt in brown that said Hoskins on it led a dappled mare.

"Can I help you?" she asked.

"I'm Ash Jericho. I'm looking for Danielle." I was tempted to add in that I was from Beauvoir

Farms, but likely the woman knew we hadn't raised horses in decades.

"You found her," Danielle said, changing her stance from just pausing to stopping. The dapple started looking for some grass to nibble on. She wasn't saddled. "Thinking of getting Beauvoir Farms back into shape? Maybe try raising a couple of stakes winners?"

I smiled and shook my head. "I don't know anywhere near enough even to hire people to do that."

Danielle raised an eyebrow. Either she was curious about why I was there or because she'd never heard anyone admit to not knowing everything there was to know about horses.

"I was out at the Willard barn when they found the body. I was wondering if you'd heard if that was your missing groom," I said.

Danielle shook her head. "Don't really expect the cops to come by and share that with me. Might be in charge herc, but I'm not the money person, you know. Not the big boss, just the little girly boss."

She made like she might spit but then didn't. It seemed like the natural act of someone who once chewed tobacco.

"It was worth a shot," I said. "It's been a hectic week for me. First finding Layla Wiltshire and then that body, although at least I didn't see the whole body there."

"Of course, everyone knows that Layla was insulting me and the horses I care for," Danielle said. "Like I go around beating the horses and hurting them. Idiot woman has no idea what kind of money goes into these guys. Neglecting them would be beyond idiocy. Anyone works here loves horses and knows them, too. Big boss checks backgrounds. I interview and double check references. You don't work here without two glowing references and two checks. The groom that disappeared? He had good references from north of here. I even called when he went off. His old boss couldn't believe it. Said it wasn't like him. I tend to believe them."

"Was he around long enough to get friendly with anyone? Or maybe get on the wrong side of someone?" I asked.

"You sound like a cop. Probably better than the cops who came by. Didn't ask me anything that formal, you know?"

I smiled at her, hoping that we were bonding. I didn't agree with her exactly. I knew that Byron would have asked plenty of questions. Sometimes he figured it was what he got when he didn't ask that was more important.

"Barry wasn't too talkative. He talked a bit to me and to Rip, one of farriers. Not sure how close they were, but I saw Barry hanging with Rip more than anyone else." Danielle shrugged and started to turn.

"Who you think murdered Layla Wiltshire?" I asked. I filed away that the groom's name was Barry.

"Someone with more guts than I got," Danielle said, turning. "Don't think I don't thank them before bed, either. They did the world a favor."

With that she led the horse off to the barn, away from me. The mare gave a nice tail swish, making a final statement.

"The farm is private, so if we're done…" Danielle didn't even turn to see if I'd leave.

But she was right. I didn't need to get in trouble for hanging out on private property where I'd finished my business. It was also clear that I wasn't going to get to come back there. I'd have to go back home to our barn and see if Jaci knew a farrier named Rip that I might talk to. Besides, I was supposed to be meeting Cheri for lunch. I needed to check in to see if she'd texted.

I hurried back to my car in time to see Byron Cabot getting out of his car.

"Fancy meeting you here," he said.

"Was the body the groom that went missing?" I asked, coming over to him.

"Was that what you were doing here? Asking

if they knew?" he asked. There was an edge to his voice.

"I figured I found the body. I didn't want to bother you."

"You also knew I wouldn't answer." Byron put his hands on his hips, daring me to contradict him.

"I knew you wouldn't answer," I said. I hoped that he'd leave the rumors about Danielle and Layla out of it.

"It was. Barry Ludwin," Byron said calmly. "Matched prints. He got printed when he got hired for a job up north. We got them back just a bit ago. I'm going to go talk to the owner and his head groom."

I nodded. I hoped that Danielle wouldn't give me away. I had a feeling she wasn't going to unless asked. She didn't seem too inclined to want to help anyone in authority.

"I'll leave you to it," I said.

Byron nodded. "You need to stay out of this. You might not be in the middle of it like last time, but you're definitely on the periphery. Don't put yourself in the center. You might not be as lucky as you were."

"I'll remember that." I turned to go, realizing that Byron was right. What if all my questions led someone to think I knew more than I did? I thought back to the people I'd talked to over the last few days and the questions I had asked. I could easily have a target on my back now. I shuddered realizing what I had done.

Chapter 23

It began to rain as I drove home. The drops started big and thick and tapered off only to pour down half a mile later. The drumbeat on the roof forced me to turn up the volume on my music. I had barely done that when the water started coming down in sheets so thick, I practically had to pull over. Fortunately, I know the roads and was able to continue on, though driving slowly and cautiously.

The rain had mostly stopped by the time I got to the house. I decided to go on past the main entrance and head to the barn. I didn't want to go walking out there if it decided to pour, again.

It would keep me busy until I heard from Cheri. She must have had a long night with Travis. I couldn't begrudge her that.

Normally, when I visited the barn, I walked along the drive that would curve back behind the carriage house and garage. The drive was wide enough for one and a half cars and shaded by trees on either side. Once past the garage, the pavement turned to gravel. Walking there was pleasant. Driving was less so due to how narrow it was.

I'm not sure that when the drive was made that anyone had ever planned for cars. It was the way the family would access their horses and that was it. Gram could have widened it, but she'd not wanted to tempt the boarder owners to use our private drive, back when the private gate stayed open during the day and someone had to manually go out and close it as night fell.

Passing the house and using the second entrance, the drive was paved, though it needed to be redone, and wider. It curved back around towards the barn, the way sheltered by trees. Even the split rail fences that lined it had bushes in front of them, making the way seem like the entrance to a garden.

As always, the barn was filled to capacity. Apparently, there was even a waitlist. I hadn't known this, but Jaci was well known for how she handled the horses. Gram had been lucky to get her when she had decided to open the barn up for boarders.

It started to pour just as I pulled into one of

the parking spaces. I waited in the car watching the drops come down, hitting the leaves of the huge tulip poplar that sat between the parking area and the barn. The tree had been there as long as I could remember, and it was always a sign I was home. Of all the things I had missed about the landscape of Kentucky when I was living in the west, this particular tree was the one I had missed most.

Tall and broad with the distinctive tulip leaves of the tree, it stood nearly a hundred feet. About halfway up it angled slightly to the left, but overall, it was in perfect shape. Gram had had an arborist out a few years back to make sure it was healthy. It would not be good if it fell on the barn.

There were others of its ilk out in the pastures, but none were quite as tall as this one nor so distinctive.

When the rain slowed to a drizzle, I got out and hurried over to the barn. There were three low concrete steps between the parking area and the packed dirt lane where the horses would walk out towards one of the pastures.

The long barn, standing two stories in height, the second floor having an apartment over the offices at one end and general storage in the rest, was painted cream with pale peach trim. It was an unusual look but one that Gram had liked. It was one place where my grandfather had indulged her.

I liked the look because it was different. Tara Morrow, one of our long-term boarders, was carrying a bucket towards her horse's stall. Though the lights were on in the barn, the gray clouds made it dark inside.

"Hi, Tara." I waved and turned down the long row. There were horse stalls on my left. The right side of the barn was open for a couple of yards before the stalls appeared there as well. Some of the horses had their heads out, checking out what was going on. Others were in their stalls doing horsey types of things.

I got to the end of the hay-covered walk and went through an arched door. There was an office to my left, with a door that was open. Jaci was standing up looking at something, her back to me.

The office itself was narrow but long from side to side, like two horse stalls put together. On the wall with the door were low file cabinets that held records for the years the farm was in service for breeding. A wooden desk in a darkish pine sat facing the door. It wasn't a huge desk, but it was still good sized with drawers on the left side, one a file drawer. A laptop computer sat on the desk.

A wide window behind the desk let in light and there were bookshelves on the wall to my right. The shelves were filled with a plethora of what-nots and a few trophies, none of them important enough to display behind glass. There were books on horses lining some shelves and plenty of photos of my grandparents.

"Hey," I said.

"Oh, hey," she said, turning. "Did you need something? I think Darryl is in the barn."

Darryl was the part-time groom who came in to help so Jaci could take time off. He was a knowledgeable kid, but he was still a high school student working weekends and some evenings, keeping the barn shipshape. While I would trust him with questions about the horses, Jaci was the person who was most suited to answer my questions.

"No, just wanted to say hi to you," I said, "and ask if you know the farrier named Rip. I heard he was a friend of Barry Ludwin."

"Barry?" Jaci said. There was something about her stance that made me think she was stalling for time. She knew something though she didn't want to say. "I've heard that name."

"He was the groom that went missing over at Hoskins." I waited while Jaci thought about something. She put down a binder of stuff on the wooden desk that sat in front of the window.

"No." Jaci paused. Her long brown hair was always back in a braid and it swished a little as she walked around. She was in blue jeans and a pink long-sleeved t-shirt and a worn blue fleece vest over it. The vest was mostly unzipped, as if she'd been taking it off before she started looking for something else. "I heard the name in some other context. Can't remember what, though."

I waited.

Jaci rolled her eyes looking at the corner of the room. "It'll come to me later on."

"I guess he was a friend of a farrier named Rip," I added, reminding her that I was looking for different information.

"Everyone knows Rip," Jaci said, smiling. "He's really just an apprentice, but he has a way with horses and with people. I think it's his enthusiasm for his job."

"Do you have a last name?" I asked, hoping to look him up.

Jaci shook her head. "But he'll be here tomorrow morning. Blackjax and two of our boarders need shoes."

I mentally went through my Monday schedule. I tended to have more patients on Mondays, but I didn't have anyone first thing. They were all clustered later in the day.

"If you remember why you know Barry's name, let me know, okay?" I said.

"I will. I wish I remembered why I did." Jaci was frowning when I left, pensive about the whole thing. She left the binder she'd been holding and wandered out to into the barn proper after me like she was looking for something.

Glancing back before heading out into the drizzle, I wondered what had her so distracted. Normally Jaci was with it, but something more than just the name of a groom was distracting her. Thinking back, I should have asked her more about it.

Chapter 24

The next morning, I was up and dressed early to head back out to the barn. Rip was scheduled to be there early and even though I only paused long enough to grab some coffee before walking over, their truck was already parked in the lot. The day was clearer than yesterday with blue skies brightening on the horizon, pink streaks still in view. The green of the trees seemed particularly bright under the morning sunshine. If I were a photographer, I'd have been having a heyday.

The musky scent of the horses mixed with the fresh clean scent of grass after a hard rain. I breathed deeply of that while I walked, carrying my coffee in a commuter mug with a cover. Who needed the caffeine when you had this?

Birds chirped here and there. The leaves rustled as an early squirrel moved about.

Bill Moss was our regular farrier, and I recognized his deep baritone voice as soon as I heard it. He was talking to someone, probably Jaci, quiet and calm as always. I had heard that Bill could get riled, but I'd never seen it. I can't say that meant anything considering I was so rarely out in the barn. Perhaps me not being a regular meant he was always on his best behavior.

"Morning, Ash," Jaci said, turning. Today's t-shirt was green and white striped. Everything else looked the same.

"Morning," I said.

Bill stood over by Marty's horse, Blackjax, talking to him. His tools were out, but he wasn't doing the work. He ran his hands down Blackjax's nose while someone else did the work.

Bill was a tall man, though slender, which belied the depth of his voice, at least in my mind. He had on work pants and boots. His face, lightly lined, had crinkles that went upwards, suggesting he was a smiler more than a frowner. His close-cropped hair was light brown and now shot through with gray. I remembered him when I was a kid and his light brown hair had been free of the gray. We were all getting older.

I glanced over at the other man who was actually doing the shoeing. It had to be Rip. He was young with blond hair so pale it looked white. It had just enough gold in it that I didn't think it was dyed that color. His eyes were blue and his eyebrows were almost as fair. Freckles dotted his nose and across his cheeks. I wondered how easily his skin burned.

"I heard you had a few questions for Rip," Bill said.

I nodded. "Heard he was friendly with Barry Ludwin. I was hoping to learn more about Barry."

"I heard you found his body," Bill said lowering his voice a bit, leaning towards me where I stood. Jaci cocked her head a little looking at me, waiting for an answer. It seemed like she was a little more interested than normal, but maybe she just wanted to know more about Barry.

"Sort of," I said. "I found something in the Willard barn and called the police. They found the body, thank heavens. I had found Layla not long before. One body is enough for me."

Bill nodded. "I can't imagine that Barry's body would have been pretty."

I waited.

"Barry was a good guy. Came down from up north, you know," Rip said. "He seemed sort of lonely, you know? He said he met this woman he kind of liked but wasn't sure about her. Guess he was worried about what his family would think.

She was a bit older than he was, you know?" Rip was looking up from his work.

Blackjax snorted a little and fidgeted like he didn't want his front leg held while people were talking.

Rip patted him on the side and leaned his head against his shoulder, and Blackjax calmed. Only then did Rip let go of the leg.

"Did the woman have a name?"

Rip shrugged. "He said he didn't want to kiss and tell, you know? I did hear that he found out something about her family that they didn't want getting out. I'm not sure what, you know? The woman didn't seem to care, though. It was some cousin of hers that was pretty pissed off."

"Really?" I asked.

This was all looking a lot like Andy was back in the picture. I wondered what Barry might have known. It had to have been Layla that Barry was obliquely referring to.

Rip went on about families and how it seemed like Barry's friend had a really bad one. I knew I was jumping to conclusions, but it made sense. Layla was older than Barry. Given how horrible everyone thought she was, family issues would have been an understatement. It's not like she'd have gone around saying she was a horrible person no one wanted to talk to.

I let Rip talk, filtering what he was saying,

trying to get to what he knew about Barry and the woman.

"Any reason at all anyone would want to hurt him?" I asked.

"What I told the police, you know?" Rip said. I was getting tired of his "you know," but I bit back my annoyance. "I think it was that woman's cousin. Everyone liked Barry and he wouldn't hurt anyone. He had a bit of money socked away so he could entertain a little more than usual, but he liked the work, liked Hoskins a whole lot. Only had good things to say about them."

That was strange if Layla was bad mouthing Danielle.

"I think he even had a bit of a crush on the head groom there," Rip said. "Course everyone knows Danielle has a girlfriend."

I smiled. Well, that could be a reason for Layla to start in on Danielle. Her young man had liked another woman, assuming Barry had been Layla's young man.

"Did anyone else know he liked Danielle?"

"Nah," Rip said. "It was just a sort of a crush, you know? I mean he wouldn't even admit it, but you could sort of hear it when he said her name. But I guess only I would, you know, because I was the only one who was, like, that good of a friend to him."

When Rip was done telling me what he knew,

I thanked him for his time. I hurried back to the house to get ready to go into the clinic to see patients. I had five people back to back, and it made me feel like a real acupuncturist again. I loved busy Mondays.

Driving to the office, I thought about what I'd learned. Certainly, jealously could have played into Layla's talk about Danielle and Hoskins farm. It still left questions about who would murder Barry and Layla.

Plus, there was the missing Evan. And Andy who was also entangled with Layla, which brought him back into the circle. I had no doubt that he had some level of involvement. I just didn't know what.

When I got to the office, there were no bodies and no group of people discussing dead bodies out front. I did see that Colleen's car was in her usual space, so she was getting the chiropractic office set up and ready for Duncan. I allowed myself a trace of envy for someone who had help. I quickly banished it and reminded myself that I needed to be thankful that I had an office and patients at all.

After the last year, I should know better than anyone that nothing is guaranteed in life.

My Monday patients had all become pretty regular. I was moving a couple of them out from every two weeks to once a month. I loved that because it meant they were getting better. I hated it because I needed new patients.

Fortunately, I had someone call about foot pain and I scheduled them for the next day. My schedule might not be full, but at least it remained steady.

A few people asked about Layla, realizing that she had been found outside my clinic. Unfortunately, none of them knew anything except for Mrs. Bates, my oldest patient, who suffered from arthritis in her knees.

I was finishing making her appointment for the next week. She could have gone every other, but she worried that her pain would come back and she wasn't ready to try going out another week.

"I love gardening so," she said. Her hair was gray and curled softly around her face, which was so wrinkled that her eyes almost got lost in them. Her nose was rounded and petite, and at one time I would guess she'd been a beautiful woman. All she needed to be one of those little garden gnome statues come to life was a pointed blue or red hat.

She'd always been short, but age had stooped her over a bit and she walked with a slight limp even though we worked on her knees regularly.

"It's a wonderful way to get outside," I said.

"I tried some of that CBD oil that Layla recommended. I swear I got sick just smelling it, and it didn't do a thing for my knees. She wasn't pleased when I told her that, either." Mrs. Bates flashed me one of her smiles that made me think of the woman she had probably been thirty years ago.

I thought I'd heard someone else had gotten sick on something Layla had recommended, or had that just been a rumor?

"That's too bad," I said. "I'm surprised it made you sick. I know that not everyone does well on it, but the fact that it made you sick…?"

"It wasn't just CBD oil," Mrs. Bates said. "She mixed it with her own herbal decoction, which was supposed to be more healthful. All I can say is that it certainly wasn't for me. It was kind of her to think of me even if it was misguided. Before you, no one really had any hope for someone like me."

"Well, I'm glad I can get you back to gardening. Are you planting now?"

Of course she was, and Mrs. Bates was only too happy to tell me about the annuals she was putting into her front garden bed and the fact that her tulips were all coming up beautifully.

It made me think that I should garden a little more.

As she left, I wished I'd made a better note of who else had gotten sick taking Layla's herbal remedies. There could be something there.

Chapter 25

Back home, after eating dinner with Daisy, I went upstairs to read for a bit before watching some television. I was sitting on the edge of the bed, starting to get comfortable, when Penelope Blue came in. Whenever she makes an appearance, I know that there's likely to be something important going on, particularly when she gets up close to me.

The little ghost cat made to head-butt me, though I felt nothing except the slightest chill against my hip. Then she leaped down onto the floor and looked back at me.

I followed her. I expected her to lead me to Gram's room, thinking there perhaps I'd be able to see my grandmother and ask her a question. Instead, Penelope Blue headed down the stairwell to the front room. Daisy was in the great room when I came down the stairs, watching a movie with a low, sad song that made me want to cry. My aunt loves romance movies. I figured this one was no exception.

I often watch with her, but I hadn't been in the mood. Maybe later we'd settle in on the large overstuffed sofa and watch something funny. There were a number of good shows that we were binge watching from Netflix and Amazon Prime.

I also knew I ought to call Cheri. She'd texted me cancelling lunch on Sunday. She'd said she was tired. We'd talked about connecting today, but it had slipped my mind. I had a feeling I was going to hear about it later when I told her what I'd learned, especially if any of this ended up being important.

Penelope Blue led me across the kitchen and then stopped at the door. I opened it. Penelope Blue followed me and stood at the edge of the step. She'd had never gone outside as a living cat, and I'd never seen her outside as a ghost, though she sometimes had come to visit me in the carriage house. She trotted through the darkening evening down towards the carriage house, her feet almost touching the ground.

I followed, wondering what she wanted. This was definitely unusual. More unusual, I mean, than just seeing a ghost cat and knowing you had to follow her.

The night wasn't too cool, for which I was grateful. I hadn't been wearing a sweater when I'd come down, and Penelope Blue hadn't warned me that I would need a jacket. I worried that if I went in to grab one, she'd disappear.

It hadn't rained at all that day and there were no clouds to cover the emerging stars or the sliver of the moon that shown in the sky. It was a pretty pleasant walk. I'd have enjoyed it if I wasn't so curious about what Penelope Blue wanted to let me see.

The barn was up ahead. I saw lights upstairs in Jaci's rooms. There were also lights downstairs in the main part of the barn. It wasn't that late, but it was getting there, so I was a little surprised. I didn't see a veterinary truck around, so no one was nursing a sick horse through the dark hours, or, at least if they were, the horse wasn't sick enough to have the vet out yet.

Penelope Blue paused by the door, not going in. I paused as well.

The cat moved along the side of the barn, placing me out of sight of anyone who looked out of the open door. She then sat down and proceeded to wash a paw. I listened, wondering what was going on, but I heard nothing but a few snorts and sniffs from a couple of the horses.

I waited. Penelope Blue sat there washing, moving from her paw to her belly. Even though the night wasn't cold, I started to feel a little chilled. Standing around in the shadows trying to remain quiet doesn't keep you very warm.

The cat stood up suddenly, as cats do, and stretched her back, arching and then lowering it down. As she sat and looked, I heard Jaci talking.

"Look, we can't hide things here anymore. Mrs. Beauvoir wasn't paying very close attention, and Morgan didn't know what to look for, not out in the barn. It used to be easy to avoid Martina, but Ash lives here and so does her aunt. One of them is bound to notice, not to mention the fact that Ash is sticking her nose into everything. She's been asking about Layla like crazy. I put her on to Barry to see what she'd do. She was right there, even went so far as to talk to Danielle and ended up talking to Rip."

There was silence. Jaci must be on the phone.

"Not in my apartment. Layla was perfect for pushing that stuff because she had no clue. Even if she did, she probably wouldn't have cared if she thought people might get help from it…"

"No." Jaci snapped after whoever had cut her off.

There was a bit of silence.

"There is no way Ash is going to sell drugs out of her clinic. She takes her work seriously, and she's nosey as hell. Besides, it's not like she needs the money. Layla did."

I bit back a gasp. Jaci sounded as if she were selling drugs. Perhaps with Layla or setting Layla up. She even set me up to ask about Barry. It sounded as if that was a test to see what I would do. My fists clenched.

I really wanted to run inside and confront her. Penelope Blue sat there glaring at me.

I felt the chill creeping into my body again. The cat was probably right. I shouldn't go running in there. Who knew what Jaci would do? I remembered Byron's warning. I'd have to call him after I slipped back to the house.

"Andy didn't mean to hurt Barry, you know that," Jaci said. "He's got that damned temper and he couldn't help himself when Barry lost that shipment."

Which suggested Andy killed Barry. Did he then kill Layla? How deep into this was Jaci?

I really needed to call Byron.

I heard Jaci still walking down the stalls. The lights were going off.

"Look. I can't help you. It's too much and I don't want to lose this job." Jaci said. The area around me darkened as she turned off the final set of lights on the far end of the barn and started down the aisle between the horses, probably heading to her office and her apartment. I wondered who she was talking to.

I breathed out.

Penelope Blue gave me a long look. When the final lights turned off on this end of the barn, leaving only the emergency lights, she gave a cat huff and faded out. She'd done her part.

I stayed where I was, listening to the horses inside, wondering if Jaci was still up and what she was doing. Blackjax was just inside to the right. There was no reason for me not to go to the barn at all. Still, after what Jaci had said about me, I doubted she'd believe I'd just come over to the barn to visit a horse.

I bit my lip. I wanted to touch something Jaci touched, like that binder. It might tell me something.

After hemming and hawing, I stepped away from the barn onto the main path. I walked into the main aisle and started looking for a light. After all, if I was supposed to be there, I'd do that, right?

Before I found the switch, the main overhead lights came on again. Jaci was standing at the far end of the barn.

"Can I help you with something, Ash?" she asked. There was no trace of her usual friendliness in her tone.

Chapter 26

I walked into the barn, trying to look more confident that I felt. Had Jaci seen me out there, huddling by the side of the barn? It was certainly possible she was just pissed off from the phone call I'd overheard. Penelope Blue was nowhere around to give me any clues.

The barn smelled of hay and horses. It was warmer than outside, the heat of the heavy animals keeping the place from getting too chill. One of the horses down the row blew out his breath and stepped to one side, slightly knocking into the wall, making an echo.

I let my hand rest on the door near Blackjax's stall. "I needed to get out and move a little," I said. "I haven't done as much as I normally do, and I need to get back into walking. I thought I'd visit Blackjax. Is that a problem?"

Jaci bit her lip and then looked down. "No. I just wasn't expecting anyone. It's starting to get late. Even our evening folks have gone. I thought maybe you were an intruder. It happens sometimes."

I knew it did. It occurred to me that perhaps Jaci selling drugs on the property, or at least storing them, could have been one of the reasons that we periodically had intruders. Were they looking for her stash?

If Jaci wasn't selling the drugs, no one would know the drugs were there, though. We were certainly close enough to town that someone without a home might see the barn as a good place to stop and rest.

"I didn't mean to disturb you." I waited by Blackjax's stall, not wanting to look as if I were turning tail, though I felt like I wanted to. This wasn't the woman I thought I knew. She'd been a rock when Gram died, and even when Marty had died, she'd been on my side. Now I didn't know.

"I was just heading upstairs," Jaci said. "I'll see you in the morning. Can you show yourself out without the main lights?"

"I can," I said.

The main lights went off and once again I was in the dimness lit only by the emergency lights.

Fortunately, it was warm enough that the main doors were left open. Jaci was upstairs, and Gram had never felt that the barn needed to be locked up tight. The property was gated, after all. Sadly, it might be a rule I had to change.

Blackjax was clearly settled. He barely acknowledged I was there. If Daisy had come out, no doubt he'd have been nuzzling her, hoping for treats. He didn't know me nearly well enough. If Jaci had tried to hurt me, I doubt I could have counted on him to get involved. Clearly my main animal protectors were ghosts.

I waited by the stall, listening as Jaci climbed the stairs. I waited a bit before I went anywhere. I tried not to be too quiet, which might set her off, but tried to keep my destination unfocused, as if I were just wandering around.

When I felt as if I done enough wandering, I went a bit more quietly towards the office. The door was closed but not locked, thank heavens.

I opened it slowly, listening for any creaks or squeaks. None. Jaci kept the place in good repair then. I looked around at the shapes in the dim light. I was happy to see she had left the binder on the desk—at least I hoped it was the same one. I had left my phone behind, so I couldn't use that for a flashlight to look closer. Nor did I want to tempt fate and turn on the overhead light.

I let my hand brush the binder and pushed away my automatic psychic protection.

I saw notations about boarders and horses. The thoughts behind the horses felt masculine, and I knew those weren't Jaci. Then I felt a sort of secretiveness, a hiding. Fear. A desire for more money. Anger at someone, frustration. And then an idea, something that was thrilling, but there was anxiety, too.

A woman was there, talking, discussing something. She was in shadow. I wasn't sure if it was Jaci I was seeing or someone else. I couldn't even tell if the memories belonged to a man or a woman. It did feel a bit more feminine, though I couldn't have said why. This memory, though, wasn't an old one.

I saw the sun shining into the room and a shadowy female figure pacing the office. They were waiting, excited about something new.

I saw someone else, someone I didn't know. The face flashed in front of me for only an instant. My mind fixated on blue eyes, the color of the sky. Heavy lids threatened to keep my eyes from seeing the color. Heavy features made up the face. Then everything was gone. Just gone. Black.

Even the vision.

I pulled my hand off the binder, wondering about the abrupt stop. It was cold in the office.

I was having a hard time seeing and I turned

to leave the room. Gooseflesh popped up on my arm. The air felt damp. I thought I smelled something burning. I worried about the horses, hurrying out, wondering how I could be so cold if there was a fire.

Behind me I thought I heard someone say, "Help me." I turned to see who was there, but the office was covered in a mist. Just like what had happened after I had read for Elle. What was going on? Who exactly needed help and how was it they were reaching out to me in this way?

The fog started fading out. The burning smell went away. Now all I could smell was the thick, musky scent of horses and hay. No one was in the office.

I started down the aisle. I was leaving the barn when I heard a car drive up, but saw no lights. I paused, looking out. I heard a door, opened carefully. No car light came on. The door was closed with the same level of muffled sound. Whoever it was, they didn't want to be seen or heard.

I went back inside and slipped into Blackjax's stall. He stirred, probably annoyed that I was bothering him so late. Sensing someone he knew who wasn't actively trying to wake him, he settled, though I felt his muscles less relaxed than they'd been moments ago. He was clearly awake and waiting with me while we both wondered what was going on.

Chapter 27

I listened for the sound of someone coming into the barn as I huddled down behind Blackjax. The horse was kind enough not to make any sound.

I felt the tension in his muscles, tension that hadn't been there when I'd come into the stall where he'd been snoozing. He knew something was off. The flick of his ears and the way he moved his head said that he was assessing the situation.

I breathed in the thick musky scent of his body. The movements outside were shadows against the wall with only the dim emergency lights on.

I heard someone come down the steps from upstairs. Had to be Jaci. Maybe the stranger was the person on the other end of the phone. The heels of Jaci's boots tapped on the cement floor, only slightly muffled by the hay on top of it.

"You got it?" Male voice, youngish.

"You see Ash?" Jaci asked. "She was here nosing around. Not sure what she was up to."

I didn't hear the response. I was tempted to move a little to see out, but even though Jaci hadn't turned on the overheads, I was worried about being noticed.

"Just you," the guy said.

I wasn't familiar with the voice. It wasn't Andy.

"It's out in my car. This can't keep going on like this. It's why I contacted Barry. Mrs. Beauvoir kept an eye on the place, but I could get around her. She wasn't quite so nosey. Ash is a whole different case. Too bad that Rick guy went and killed Marty. Marty wouldn't have known something was up if you waved a brick under her nose." Jaci laughed at that.

I gritted my teeth. Marty wasn't exactly the most observant of people, but she had a real issue with drugs. It's one reason why I never believed her murder had been suicide. It didn't fit.

"Yeah, well, Andy's being watched by the police thanks to his boyfriend going missing. Any word?"

"Nah. I think he's well aware of what happens

if he turns up. Andy should never have paid off the freakin' credit card bill. It just brought attention to the money he shouldn't have had. Idiot." Jaci sounded annoyed.

"His mother is still looking for him. I don't know why he hasn't turned anyone in."

"I don't think he has any proof, just his word, which if we all say different or point fingers at him, particularly with Barry's body turning up, well… there's more of us than of him, right?"

I really wished I had my cell phone to record this. When had Jaci become a drug dealer? She'd been this nice woman I'd known for a number of years. We'd paid her well. She cared about the horses. She could have moved on if she wanted to stay with racehorses, but she said she'd been happy here.

Blackjax snuffed and then sneezed. He didn't stand up.

I ducked down behind him, hoping that my clothing wasn't too bright and wouldn't attract attention if anyone looked in the stall.

"Just go get the stuff. Leave the keys on the desk in the office. I'll be upstairs. Easier to deny knowing anything if Ash comes back out and wonders what's going on."

"She'll regret seeing me," the man said. I hid down behind Blackjax, wondering who that was. I listened as they left. I heard Jaci go upstairs. The other person walked through the stables, passing my hiding place, and then out into the night.

I waited for a bit, letting my hands rub against Blackjax's warmth. He gave a slight huff which was answered by one of the other horses in the barn.

I leaned back against the wall, counting. I didn't want to leave too soon, to be caught and perhaps asked what I was doing there.

Time moved slowly past. I heard Jaci moving around upstairs. Still, I waited with Blackjax. I let my eyes close and I drifted for a little while. When Blackjax laid back and relaxed, pushing up against the wall, I stood and stepped around him.

He gave one tired look at me before laying his head back down. I slipped out of his stall and hurried back to the house. I needed to call Byron. It was too bad that Penelope Blue couldn't have told me to take my cell phone.

The night was cooler than it had been. It was no longer going on night, but full dark, the moon slightly obscured by a floating cotton candy cloud. I crossed my arms and walked as quickly as I could back towards the house, hoping that Jaci didn't just happen to look out and see me.

We had security around the barn, so if I asked to see the tapes, chances were I'd see who had come in. If Jaci looked, she'd see me and know that I left after her chat with the mysterious man I hadn't seen. I really needed to get back and tell Byron.

I broke into a light jog. I thought I heard someone pacing me, but I didn't dare look back. I pictured the man I'd heard in the barn, thinking him as a big, strong football player ready to tackle me.

I started to run, which meant that by the time I reached the side door of the house I was winded. There were no lights on inside, so I'd been gone a fair amount of time. Daisy had no doubt given up on me. The light over the side door was on but the main door was locked. Morgen knew I was outside but expected me to have my key.

I didn't.

All I could hear was my ragged breathing as I rang the bell, feeling only a little a guilty that I was waking someone up, probably Morgen.

I thought I felt something on my shoulder but when I turned, no one was there. The footsteps had been a trick of sound as I ran between the trees and along the hard-packed dirt until I reached the concrete drive nearer the house. No one was following me, though that didn't mean no one knew what I had heard.

I was shivering by the time Morgan got to the door, though I knew he'd likely hurried.

"Miz Ash?" he said. "No key?"

"I didn't expect to be out so late," I said.

He looked me up and down and gave a quick look outside to be sure no one was following me.

"Are you all right? I can make some cocoa if you like?"

I shook my head. I wasn't that cold. Just scared and much of that had been me scaring myself.

"Thanks, though," I said. I hurried up the stairs to find my phone. I was going to call Byron.

Even if the security footage in the barn didn't have audio, and I was pretty sure it didn't, I had to tell the police. When they found Evan Mabry, he could corroborate my story. At least I hoped he could.

I hurried to my room and found my phone. I noticed I'd missed five phone calls, all from Cheri. I frowned, wondering what was going on.

Just as I was taking a moment to debate calling her first, the phone rang. Cheri again.

"What's up?" I asked answering.

"Where have you been?" she demanded.

"I was out at the barn," I said.

"This late?" she asked.

"Long story. And I'll tell you when we go to lunch tomorrow, okay?" I said. Cheri and I usually do lunch on Tuesdays, and then she normally shows up, unlike our on again, off again Sunday lunch. This week we'd talked about meeting at the local deli. It was a small place which sold a variety of sandwiches and they were actually known for their quiche. It surprised me that it did so well in a town the size of Seales, but between having something common like sandwiches, and something different, like quiche, as well as having an assortment of mini cupcakes for those who wanted a small dessert, meant they did okay.

"You won't believe what I heard. I was out with Travis at the Brewery tonight and I heard two of the waitresses talking. One of them was saying she had talked to Evan Mabry and he was terrified for his life. I guess he's afraid of his husband but doesn't want to go to the police because he doesn't want to have to testify against him. The girls are young enough to think this is so romantic and all and I get that, but it sounds more like a domestic violence type situation, you know? Where someone can't get out and are afraid to tell and all," Cheri said. "I hoped they'd say where he was or give me some sort of clue, but I didn't get that lucky."

I sat down on the bed. "That's too bad. I think I need Evan to help me with something I have to tell Byron."

"What was it?" Cheri asked.

I gave her the overview of what I'd heard at the barn.

"Wow. Just wow. Call Byron right now. I'll talk to you at lunch unless you're down at the station or something."

"Lord, I hope not," I said. "I have patients in the morning."

"Still…" Cheri said before ringing off.

I punched in Byron's number. It didn't even ring, just went straight to voicemail. I told him to call me as soon as he could. Then I changed into sweats, intending to rest while I waited for him to call. I did not expect to fall asleep until dawn.

I woke to Penelope Blue sitting on my chest, sending a chill through me and into my heart, forcing me up. Something was very wrong.

Chapter 28

Now that I was obviously awake, I smelled faint traces of smoke. I sat up quickly, forcing Penelope Blue off the bed. She stood beside the bed and looked at me, her mouth opening and closing like she was meowing at me.

From beneath the pale cream shades that covered the windows, I saw the faintest pink dawn. The smell of smoke was faint. Either it was outside or it wasn't a very big fire.

I had fallen asleep in my sweats. My phone was on my chest, the battery at about a quarter. I took it with me as I slipped my feet into shoes and hurried downstairs.

I didn't hear Win in the kitchen or Daisy or Morgan. Something was going on. I hurried even more.

The smoky smell was stronger on the main floor and I saw flames outside. The carriage house.

I ran out the side door. Morgan was already there. He had the garden hose spraying water over the bushes around the house. Win had another hose and was attempting to fight the fire. I didn't see Daisy.

"Have you called the fire department?" I yelled.

"Already done!" Morgan yelled back. He didn't even look. I hurried back to the kitchen. There were buckets there. I started filling one of them in the big sink. I grabbed another and ran to the bathroom behind the great room and started that filling in the bathtub. I'd toss what water I could on the front plants so that Morgan could concentrate on the side closest to the barn.

By the time I was running out with the first bucket from the kitchen sink, sirens were blaring loudly outside. Air brakes hissed as the fire engine slowed to make the turn into our driveway. I ran back to the house to turn off the faucet in the bathroom now that help was here.

Morgan stayed to one side continuing to keep the garden soaked.

The red engine was in the drive before I reached the door to go inside. Morgan must have opened the gate in preparation for them. I'd have forgotten all about it.

I worried about Daisy, hoped she was okay. The fact that she was missing bothered me. Turning off the water, I hurried back outside, my feet barely touching the ground. I was glad I had on sweats.

Morgan was moving aside, shutting off the water as the Seales fire department got to work efficiently and quickly.

"Anyone inside?" one man called. He was wearing a heavy brownish jacket over yellow pants, a yellow helmet obscuring his face.

"Not that I know of!" Morgan called back.

"Where's Daisy?" I asked him in a quiet voice. "I can't imagine she hasn't heard the noise."

"She was the one who woke me up. She wasn't sleeping very well and was downstairs having an early morning cup when she saw smoke. She woke me to check it out and she ran off to the barn. I expect she's down there," Morgan said.

Of course. Daisy would have thought of the horses first if she wasn't certain where the smoke was coming from. When I had woken up, it was clear that the smoke was part of a fire in the carriage house. If Daisy just seen wisps of smoke, she'd have gotten Morgan to check around the big house and run off to check the barn.

If she'd been alone, the barn would have been

the more important building. I shuddered at the thought of what would happen if the barn went up. I'd heard horror stories. I was very glad not to live one.

I waited while the firemen sprayed the carriage house with water, the pressure high enough to make a difference, even though the flames were now lapping at the roof of the little place. So much for going back there to live.

I thought of the whatnots that Gram had kept there, homey decorations that visitors could enjoy. I had been the primary visitor and I had enjoyed them. It was bad enough that the place had been damaged when I'd lived there, the window broken out when Rick Darlington had tried to strangle me. Now the places was being devoured by fire.

"You working this morning, Miz Ash?" Morgan asked quietly.

"Shit, yes. I'm supposed to work." I glanced at the time. I had half an hour, but there was no way I was going to be able to concentrate, even if I could get my car out of the garage.

I looked at my phone, which was slowly dying, and hurried inside to pull up my appointment book and make some calls. Explaining to my three patients what was going on took more time than I expected, but all agreed easily to rebook. One would come the next day, another would come on Friday. The third decided to just skip a week and see how she felt. We were close to moving out every other week anyway.

No one blamed me for having a house fire. Two of them knew I lived on a farm and made sure the barn wasn't in danger. All three thanked me for letting them know. As if other business owners would have just forgotten about them.

People are good. I let myself bask in the moment of collective understanding before heading back out to watch the firemen work. Hopefully they would know what had caused the blaze.

While I was inside making calls Daisy returned. Her white mule slippers were now brown, the back of her heels equally brown. Her pale pink robe was dark either with soot or with dirt, I couldn't tell. Her hair was flying in all directions, and she'd never looked so disheveled even in those horrible days after Marty died.

Daisy saw me and her eyes lit up. I hurried over to her. "I was worried." I took her into a hug.

Daisy hugged me back, hard. "I was so worried someone had done something to the horses. Jaci was already up, thankfully, and she hadn't noticed anything. We went through the barn, though, just to make sure."

Daisy was starting to shake.

"Let's get you inside," I said quietly. "You're freezing."

It wasn't that cold any longer, not now that the

sun was up, but Daisy's robe was thin and her lower legs mostly bare. I was in sweats and a t-shirt, and if I hadn't been standing nearer to a burning building than I wanted, I would have been cold.

Daisy smiled at little and nodded. We left the firemen to their job.

Not for long.

Chilled through and looking at the mess of her outfit, Daisy immediately went upstairs to change. That left me alone downstairs. I headed back out to see what was going on.

The fire was mostly out. The carriage house wasn't being used, so nothing had been left on, so I wondered what had started the fire. It looked sad with part of the roof missing and the glass from the windows blown out. I didn't relish the idea of what would need to be done to repair it.

A particularly tall man, his dark hair slicked back either with sweat or with water, was talking to Morgan. I went over to see what was going on.

"I have to call in the arson squad, and I'll have homicide checking in. I'll need everyone in the house to stay there until you can all be interviewed."

"Homicide?" I asked.

The man looked at me, noticing me for the first time.

"There's a body in there. Do you know who was staying there?"

"No one," I said. "Normally I live there, but I haven't for some time because I was attacked there. Now I'm in the big house."

"Well, someone was there," the fireman said, not taking his eyes from mine. "And now they're dead."

Chapter 29

I wrapped my arms around myself, thinking about the dead man in the carriage house. Daisy and Win were inside. Win was cleaning up, her face blackened by smoke while she'd been trying to hose down the house. Daisy was probably making iced tea for the firemen. I had no doubt she'd be out shortly.

Morgan was standing next to me in shock. His eyes met mine, probably wondering the same thing I was. How had a dead man gotten into the carriage house? Had someone been living there and we'd not noticed? Worse, had there been a dead body inside the building for days?

I thought back to last night, trying to remember if I noticed any usual smells, but I hadn't.

It seemed like Penelope Blue would have

warned me if there was someone in there, at least if they were dead.

The sun was high in the sky. I glanced at my phone, realizing it was about time to get ready to go meet Cheri. There was no way I was going to make it, even if I hadn't been told to stick around.

"Hey, my phone's almost dead," I said.

"Are you on your way?"

"There was a fire here this morning. I'm still talking to the responders," I said. Why did firemen sound like such a childhood name for a profession? Or else a sort of stripper club kind of thing?

"Where?" Cheri asked.

"Carriage house. I don't think I'm going to make lunch. Win will probably be whipping something up here if you want to come by…"

I hadn't even finished when Cheri agreed that she was on her way. I put my phone back in my pocket. I wondered why Byron hadn't called me. I ought to call him, but that would entail going back inside and charging the phone.

He might already be on his way if the body had been reported. I wondered what he'd think of what I knew about Jaci.

I went inside to talk to Daisy and Win.

As I had thought, Daisy was busy making iced tea. Sweet, of course. That meant brewing up hot tea, dissolving sugar into it, and then putting ice in it to cool it off. Win had washed and was in a fresh outfit of khakis and button-down shirt to help.

"Cheri is coming by. We usually do lunch on Tuesday," I said. I wasn't sure how to tell them that there was a body in the carriage house.

"I'll make some soup," Win said. "I could do a quiche or maybe you won't want something so fancy?"

"I think keep it simple. The fire chief told Morgan and me there was a body in the carriage house."

Win crossed herself absently, eyes wide.

"What?" Daisy breathed. Her hands paused over the tea, staring at me.

"They said there was a body inside. I have no idea who or how. The house was locked."

"Morgan usually checks it before he turns in," Win said. "If they broke in, they were good."

We had cameras around the big house, now, too.

I'd have to look through the tape that was left. It wasn't like we sat and watched them in real time. The cameras were mostly to pick up anyone wandering around and to film them in case of a problem. Like this.

The carriage house didn't have cameras, though, so if the person had come in through the back fields and gone behind the place, the cameras would have missed them. It's not like the little place had a back door. Even the windows on that side were smaller on the main level.

I heard more cars in the drive. I hoped one of them belonged to Cheri. I looked out but saw only the police. At first, I didn't see Byron, only an officer that I expected would get the job of looking around the scene before asking questions.

Opening the side door to get a better look, I saw Byron talking to the fire chief. Hopefully he'd stay on this death even if we were linked. It wasn't like I was implicated in this, at least not right now.

I thought back to last night, having woken Morgan up after being out on the grounds late. Morgan's look came back to me. Did he think I was meeting someone in secret? My heart sunk as I realized I could be suspect even in these latest murders.

Morgan came to the door and stared at me. Once he had my attention, he cocked his head and then went into the study. I followed.

He stood in the middle of the study, the lovely turquoise colors and the bright light wood of the desks and shelves making the place a bit happier than it should have been, at least considering the conversation we were about to have. I touched one of the wingback chairs that sat in a corner and noticed that Babs was curled on the window seat. I wondered where Hellspark had taken off to. Probably Gram's room or maybe Daisy's.

"Did you know who was out there?" he asked.

"No. Did you?"

Morgan gave me a sad look. "Of course not. But I wasn't the one outside last night."

"Penelope Blue led me to the barn," I said.

Morgan brightened. He knew I could see Gram's long-deceased cat. He knew about my gift. He'd known about Gram's gift as well and was aware that Penelope Blue only showed up when something was important.

"Don't remember her ever taking Miz Beauvoir that far," he muttered.

"I heard Jaci on the phone. I think she knows something about Evan Mabry's disappearance and Layla Wiltshire's death," I said. I explained how I'd gone to the barn office to see if there was anything there that would give me clues about why. I told him about the man who arrived in the dark while I hid in the stall with Blackjax.

"I was so late because I was out there for so long," I said. "I didn't want to end up walking out when he was still there. As it was, I felt like someone was following me."

"Maybe they were," Morgan said. "Maybe the person who was in the carriage house followed you and that gave them away?"

I smiled at the old man. "You'd make a good detective."

"Except we can't just go telling the police that

you followed a ghost cat out to the barn and then decided to hang out in the barn office to see what your psychic power could tell you," Morgan pointed out.

"I could say I went for a walk. I could say I overhead Jaci say something that suggested there might be irregularities in our books, so I stayed in the office to look things over. I lost track of time. When I was leaving, I saw the truck pull up without headlights and I got scared."

Morgan nodded. "That works. Then I don't have to lie to the police, either."

A thought occurred to me. "What if the person who pulled up has been using the carriage house?"

"Or someone else. Someone who didn't want to be found." Morgan nodded at me.

I immediately thought of Evan Mabry.

The bell rang and Morgan went to get it. Byron Cabot stood on the stoop, looking sad and serious. I hitched my shoulders forward and prepared to tell my sanitized tale.

Chapter 30

I led Byron to the living room, which was the easiest place to talk and have a bit of privacy. He hadn't asked for privacy, but I had a feeling he'd want it. Police always did.

The living room in the front, across from the study, was the most formal looking room in the house. It was all creams and yellow and splashes of green. Even the sofa was cream, not something I'd have attempted. Gram was brave that way, plus she was used to having people clean-up for her, not to mention that if it did get stained, she knew she could afford a new one.

The walls were hung with hunting prints of dogs and horses. They looked like they'd have been at home in a house a hundred years older. Gram said they were my grandfather's favorites, so she kept them. I had no doubt the images also reminded her of happier times, when the family had been young and they had all had years ahead of them.

I sat in one of the cream and green club chairs and Byron took the other one. Morgan dithered a bit until Byron waved him off, telling him he'd talk to him in a minute.

"So, a fire and a body," Byron started.

I shrugged, wondering where to start. "I tried calling you last night, but you weren't around."

"Did you know about the body?" Byron asked, eyes getting wide.

"No, I would have called the main police number if I had," I said. "I overheard something that Jaci was saying in the barn." I gave him the sanitized version of my doings out there, repeating the story I'd made up at the end of my conversation with Morgan.

Byron took notes. "But you don't know who she was talking to or have anyone who can corroborate."

While Blackjax and Penelope Blue had been there, neither one of them would qualify as a witness. I shook my head.

"Morgan let me in the house when I got back. It had gotten pretty late. I was worried about the guy who had driven up with no headlights, so I dozed in Blackjax's stall. I didn't want to get caught."

Bryon nodded and then looked at me. "Was there anything specific that made you afraid?"

"Other than the content of Jaci's conversation and the fact that she clearly thought I was too nosey for my own good?" I asked.

"Just that. Why think the person visiting had anything to do with something illegal?"

"The headlights on the car were off. And he closed the door very softly. No interior light came on. I just felt there was something off and it bothered me. I might have a perfect right to be anywhere around the property, but it was dark and someone could easily have decided to shoot first and ask questions later."

It wasn't that anyone on our property went around shooting intruders. We were actually pretty nice about it, knowing that the weather can get bad and people need a place to stay inside. Even so, it would be easy enough for someone who wanted me dead to make that argument. I'd be dead so it wouldn't matter.

After Marty and Gram, I had spent some time with our attorneys creating a will. Most of the estate would go to my brother, while making sure Daisy had something to live on. While she was only a Beauvoir by marriage, Daisy had been a big part of my life. I wanted her to have something. It wasn't like she had anyone to leave it to, and anything she left behind could go to Bobbie.

It was unlikely that had something happened last night that anyone would have blamed Jaci, unless she was more careless than I thought.

Byron nodded. "Interesting information. You didn't see any lights or anything in the carriage house?"

I shook my head. "I have to admit that I was still kind of creeped out after hiding in the barn. I just wanted to get back to the house. I thought I heard someone behind me, but when I had to wait for Morgan to open the door, no one came up to me, so it must have been my imagination. I think that I would have noticed someone in the carriage house, though. I keep thinking I want to move back there, but then I remember what happened with Rick..." I trailed off. Bryon knew very well what had happened with Rick as he had been instrumental in saving me.

Byron made notes. "Did you notice the time?"

I told him I hadn't, only that it seemed later than I had expected. Maybe Morgan had noticed? I didn't say he probably had. Morgan was the type of person to notice those things.

"Can you have him come in here and talk to me?" Byron asked.

Just as I asked Morgan to go talk to Byron,

Cheri arrived. She came to the side door, barely waiting for me to answer.

"I cannot believe that you have a body on your property and all those firemen—and aren't they good-looking? That one in the front with the dark hair that's sort of curling over his forehead looks like the kind of guy I wouldn't push out of bed," Cheri said, craning her neck.

"How's Travis?" I asked, smiling.

Cheri gave me a wave. "I like him. I think he likes me. I'm not kicking him out either, but that doesn't mean I can't admire a guy from afar. Can you even imagine me with a fireman? I'd be worried half to death every time there was the tiniest fire, and I'd drive him so nuts he'd leave before we'd had any fun at all. So. Tell me about this body."

I was used to Cheri's abrupt subject changes, but I saw Daisy sort of start from her place at the table. Then she smiled and started clearing her stuff up.

"We can use the dining room," I said. "And you can join us if you like."

"Oh heavens, who wants to use that cavernous old room with only three of us," Daisy said. "A laptop is easy enough to clear away and Win can get you something. She's been making sandwiches like crazy. I think there's soup, too. Tea or lemonade?" Daisy asked Cheri.

"Sweet?"

"Naturally."

"Then sweet tea," Cheri said moving over to the table and seating herself. I joined her there.

"Well?" Cheri demanded.

Which meant that I got to tell my story yet again, this time with Daisy and Win listening in. I saw Win frown a bit when I mentioned what went on with Jaci, but she turned and took a plate of sandwiches out to the firemen before I could ask her about it.

Still, it made me wonder what she knew or thought she might know about Jaci and her drugs and perhaps even the murder. She might even know whose body was in the carriage house.

Chapter 31

I kept hoping to talk to Win, but she was staying out of my way, only bringing over sandwiches and soup. She made sure our tea was refilled as she'd flit from the kitchen off to another room. I could probably have told Cheri about my suspicions that Win knew something, but Cheri was less than tactful, sometimes. After Win had been accused of murdering my cousin, I didn't want Win to think I suspected her.

In point of fact, I didn't think Win had done anything. I thought she knew something, like perhaps overheard something. Win is young and quiet and she's often around when you don't even notice. She'd say it's because she's "the help," but in fact I always notice Morgan. I notice Win less so.

Even though she hums and sings and seems to dance through the house, it's easy to overlook her.

Jaci came to the big house at least once a week. She always sat down with Morgan and they went over the expenses and income. It didn't take long, but she would be in the house regularly. Like all of us, Jaci always had her phone. It would have been easy enough for Win to hear a conversation on that phone.

I was impatient to talk to her. Hopefully, she'd feel comfortable enough to tell Byron when he questioned her. I had no doubt we'd all get questions about what we knew about the carriage house. I hoped Win would talk to Byron if she did know something.

Cheri stayed through the afternoon. We spent the day talking in the great room. We were seated at either end of the dark green and brown sofa, shoes off, feet curled under us. The sun came though the large windows. The flat-screen TV stared at us with blank, black eyes.

Daisy left us alone, leaving to go exercise Blackjax. I had a feeling that she was leaving partly just to get out of the house and partly to make sure everything really was okay at the barn. It had been quite a scare.

After talking to everyone, Byron came into the main room and said goodbye.

"I'll be checking into Jaci," he said. "And her

background. I've never had complaints, so her involvement surprises me."

"I'd love to know how long it's been going on," I said. "It makes me angry that she was using Gram. I'd go out and fire her, but I don't want her to have an excuse to leave the area."

Byron nodded. "I have a man watching the stables, and he's been there since we talked. She's not going anywhere."

That made me feel better.

"I don't suppose you know who the body was yet, do you?" I asked.

Byron shook his head. "I'll let you know when we find out, particularly since the identity might give us an idea as to what he was doing in there."

"It couldn't be Evan Mabry, could it?" Cheri asked. "I know that Elle came and talked to Ash about what had happened to him, you know the way people always talked to her Gram about things like that."

"What way that people talked to her Gram about things like that?" Byron asked, head cocked. He looked interested but not threatened.

Cheri gave me a sort of shrug and a smile. "Miz Beauvoir could read objects. She'd touch something and she'd get impressions off of it. Sometimes feelings, sometimes seeing entire scenes of things. I think she could also see ghosts a bit too. I heard her once at Ash's birthday talking to Penelope Blue, and that cat had died quite a number of years before."

I made a mental note that Cheri was far more observant than anyone gave her credit for, particularly about psychic stuff.

"And you do it, too?" Byron asked.

My heart sank a bit. This was not what I wanted to talk about. I knew that sooner or later I was going to have to tell Cheri, but I wanted to wait and feel Byron out. I could almost hear my mother practically screaming at me to tell no one about my abilities because they'd think I was crazy. My mother had always been certain my grandmother needed therapy and then she'd let go of her delusions about being psychic.

"I guess, a bit," I said, downplaying the ability.

"A ghost cat?" Byron quirked an eyebrow.

I just smiled and shrugged. "Gram was fond of animals," I said. "Living here you got used to it."

Again with that nod and then he was off.

"Did you not want me to tell him?" Cheri said, leaning forward.

"Just that my mom always thought it was a little bit crazy," I said.

"You know, you ought to see how good you are. Let's go out to the barn and check out stuff in the office."

Leave it to Cheri to suggest the very thing I'd been doing the night before.

"I can't just run out there. I mean, they're watching Jaci."

"Yeah, but they haven't arrested her yet. Maybe you'll find something out that lets you give them more info to push her about. It's not like she's the sort of person that you can just get information from."

Clearly Jaci wasn't. She'd been good when I'd questioned her.

"Byron would tell me to leave it to the police," I said.

"Well, then..." Cheri trailed off as she rooted around for her shoes and started putting them on. "I'm going to go visit the horses. It's not like you can stop me because I'm already on the property and have reason to be there. Daisy might just be grooming Blackjax, so I can help out a bit." She looked triumphant at saying that.

I shook my head. "Then I guess I need to go with you, don't I?" I said.

"I think you do. And I think you're going to go into the office and start touching things and tell me what you see. I'll keep a look out, okay?" Cheri was nodding away as she planned my incursion. How she expected me to know what things to touch, I don't know. The office wasn't a personal space but a public one.

However, if something had happened that upset Jaci, there might something there that would resonate. The binder had a bit but not enough to tell me anything I hadn't overheard.

I did not want to do with this with Cheri. I didn't want to become her go-to psychic, but as I followed her slowly out the side door, I didn't have a way of avoiding it.

Chapter 32

It felt warm outside, the heat left over from the fire that had gutted the carriage house. The air was heavy with smoky fog. Beyond the haze, I saw clear blue skies. The day smelled like a bonfire.

Cheri and I hurried past the old carriage house, hoping no one would ask where we were going. The scene had changed from firefighters in yellow to police in black. It was bad enough to have a break-in. At least that had been easily fixed. The fire had pretty much destroyed the carriage house. The roof on the side away from the house had caved in. Even the siding looked blackened. I couldn't imagine what it looked like inside.

A few men who were clearly from the fire department were with the police and gesturing and talking. I didn't look too long. I didn't see Byron around and figured he was at the barn, probably talking to Jaci. Hopefully, Cheri and I wouldn't get in the way.

"It's amazing how many people are out and around when something burns," Cheri said quietly. "All those firefighters earlier, and now the police, and of course the smoke that's still around, like it's never ever going to go away. I can't even imagine. I'm just glad you weren't living in there."

I nodded, agreeing. We walked down the trek to the barn, the same trek I'd taken only last night. So much had changed since then. I hadn't known that I might be employing a criminal. I wasn't dealing with the loss of the place that I had thought of as home, even if I wasn't living there.

I wondered what Cheri would say if I told her why I'd really gone out there, that the cat had led me there and I'd followed. Was I crazy to see ghost cats or crazier to follow them?

There were plenty of cars in the little parking area, trucks and a few sedans. No marked police cars. I wondered how the officer was keeping an eye on Jaci. There were people talking in the barn. I saw Maria Rudyard leading her horse out to one of the trails, probably to give him a run.

"No Blackjax?" Cheri said looking in the stall.

"Daisy's probably out riding," I said. "She's been doing that a lot. I think she's bonding with him."

"Well, that's good for both of them." Cheri continued on towards the office, not letting me pause to chat with anyone for more than a hello. She was definitely not going to let me out of touching something in the office.

I suppose if I really didn't want to, I could have dug in my heels and turned back. Cheri might have started asking questions, but Jaci couldn't have done anything with so many people around. Still, I felt better that there were two of us. At least if the officers weren't around immediately, there would be two against one, or worst case, two against two.

I walked into the back of the barn where the office was. The office was across from the stairs to Jaci's apartment. Beyond that was a cross hallway that led to a large tack room, a smaller tack stall, a storage closet, and a small powder room.

Before following Cheri into the office, I took a few more steps and looked up the stairs to Jaci's place. I noticed that the door at the top was open. It was possible that the police were up there, but I didn't hear anyone moving around. Normally every footfall was obvious, even with people talking and the horses awake and having their own horsey conversations.

Maybe Jaci had already been taken in for questioning by the police. I hadn't had the impression that they were going to arrest her that quickly, though.

In the office, Cheri was sitting behind the desk, opening drawers.

"Find anything interesting for me?" I asked. I noted that the binder I had touched last night was gone. I looked around the room, studying the pictures. I looked at the books, but I couldn't imagine veterinary references would generate anything but fearful searching on the part of many owners and grooms.

"Nothing real interesting. What kinds of things work best for you?" Cheri asked, still looking.

"Anything that has strong emotions attached to it," I said. "So long as it's not living and breathing."

"Is there a way for someone to tell what sorts of things have strong emotions attached?" Cheri asked.

"Personal items usually have more emotions than, say, a business item, but it isn't always true." I walked over to the window and looked out at one of our boarders walking their horse. I sighed. Jaci would have done that if the horse needed it and the owner couldn't get there. I was going to need someone to fill in, and quickly.

In addition, I should probably go over the books a bit more closely to be sure she hadn't embezzled anything from Gram. I'd also need to be sure that our clients were getting what they had paid for. This was such a mess. Maybe taking on horse boarding wasn't such a good idea.

"I don't see anything in here. What about Jaci's personal belongings?" Cheri asked.

"Upstairs," I said. "Going upstairs would be trespassing, and even if I could argue that I own the place, it's just rude."

Cheri frowned. "What about a saddle or something like that. Doesn't she keep some stuff down here?"

I couldn't image that Jaci didn't have her own saddle. Once Marty had died, Jaci often rode Blackjax when he needed to get out. It was only recently that Daisy had realized riding was a way for her to feel closer to Marty.

I nodded, walking out of the office. It was good to be out of the office. Jaci already thought I was a snoop. No need to get caught and prove her point. Plus, what if the police wanted to investigate records? I'd have to make up a story for them. While it might not seem like it, I hated to lie.

In between the tack room and the bathroom was a small storage closet. It, too, was really Jaci's property. While I was tempted to see if it was locked, hoping that there was something personal in there, I knew very well that that room wasn't public. Besides, people went in and out of the barn all the time. Jaci wouldn't have left that room unlocked.

The small tack room on the far end had an open door. Anything in there was fair game for any of our boarders. The larger tack room had a lock. It was merely a knob that took a key rather than a heavy deadbolt.

Jaci might keep that room locked. Most of the things in there belonged to our family. Gram's old saddle was still there. Even some of Grandpa's old riding gear gathered dust in a corner. Things I ought to do something about but hadn't gotten around to.

I placed my hand on the knob, feeling the coolness of it. I didn't try for impressions. Chances were I'd get a muddle of emotions and not much else. I turned it, holding my breath.

The knob turned. The door stuck for a moment but then opened with only the slightest scraping sound.

Inside, across the back wall was a row of double shelves near the ground and hooks for bridles above. There were several blankets in the shelves, folded neatly. Plenty of bridles hung on the pegs. To my left were two rows of saddle trees. Half of them were empty. In the right corner was another saddle tree, where Grandpa had his saddle and a large plastic container covered in a horse blanket, the extent of Grandpa's leftover horse breeding program.

A table sat off to my right, a big rectangular thing with a shelf on the bottom that held a pile of old horse blankets. There was a basket to one side of the door for blankets that needed to be sent out for repair or for cleaning. A single blanket sat in the basket. Our boarders all got their own little cupboards for storing items, so these things were just things that belonged to us.

A few helmets sat on shelf above a bench on the right wall. There was just enough space to lean over and put on gear without hitting the table.

I walked into the room followed by Cheri.

I touched one of the saddles to the left. Gram's. I saw her riding, felt the wind in my hair, love for the horse she was on. I felt the strong muscles of the horse moving and the thrill of being one with her horse. The emotions were almost overwhelming to me, smelling the horsey scent and even the faint taste of gardenia which Gram loved.

I pulled out of that memory and moved on, reluctantly.

The next one had no memories or only vague ones.

I hit the jackpot with the third. I felt Jaci as if I were one with her. There was joy in riding, frustration that she had washed out as a jockey and had to take a job as a groom. Pride in a job well done. Joy and frustration woven together so tightly it wasn't possible to pull one strand without the other.

Sorrow. There was a deep pain there, a loss. I strained to see or feel what it was, but the more I pushed, the more elusive it became. Images of horses pushed away the sorrow, too many to identify even if I'd known every horse in every barn in Kentucky. It was like a parade of every horse Jaci had ever ridden or seen, a microcosm of Jaci's life —horse after horse. They were her passion, though there was another passion, a hidden one that I was almost able to catch, a fleeting glimpse like a person noticed only as they were slipping out of a room.

I was physically pulled away from the saddle.

I started to say something to Cheri only to come face to face with Jaci.

The door was closed and Jaci had a knife. Cheri was tied to the table, struggling, trying to yell through the scarf stuffed in her mouth. Apparently even being with someone wasn't enough to keep me safe from Jaci.

"Don't even think about making a noise," Jaci whispered.

Chapter 33

The knife gleamed silver in the overhead light. Cheri was still tugging at her bindings and kicking, doing what she could to make noise.

Jaci took a step and backhanded Cheri across the face while menacing me with the knife.

"Where were you?" I asked.

"I hid in the bathroom when I saw you walking back this way. I figured you were the one who told the police," Jaci snarled.

I nodded. I hated that I was sweating, that I smelled as if I were terrified. I hadn't learned anything useful, other than that Jaci loved the horses.

"Why attack?" I asked.

"Seems like it's the least I can do for payback."

"Didn't you set the fire?" I asked. "The one in the carriage house?"

Jaci shook her head. "You think I'm into everything, don't you? That's what being a gossip will get you. All I did was make a little extra letting a few drugs change hands here. That's all."

"Why?" I asked. "We paid you well. I know Gram did everything she could to treat you well. If it wasn't good enough, you're known around here. You could have worked anywhere if you wanted to be closer to racing."

Jaci shook her head. "You don't get it. I live above the friggin barn. Yeah, y'all made it nice. I could probably have talked your Gram into letting me live in your precious carriage house if I wanted. I don't doubt Miz Beauvoir would have made it up exactly like I wanted, but it still wouldn't have been mine. I want something of my own. I want to own a house. I figured if I made enough with the drugs, I could own my own place. Hell, if I worked long enough and hard enough, maybe even have some land for my own horse, rather than taking care of everyone else's."

It wasn't a huge dream. If Gram had known, she'd have bought a little house and given it to Jaci. If Jaci had asked, hell I'd have worked out a way for her to do it. We needed someone on the property near the horses, and Jaci had been a good, hard worker. The boarders all liked her, had nothing but good things to say.

I shook my head, thinking about it, feeling

hurt, wishing that she'd said something else, that she'd been unreasonable.

Cheri was still struggling.

"And so you started running drugs and killing people?" I asked.

"I never killed anyone. Did I know about it? Yeah. And it just got worse. First Andy accidentally killed Barry. Then Layla started getting all freaked out about the murder and he killed her too. Evan went into hiding..." Jaci stopped, looking at me, sadly, for a long time.

I waited, watching the knife, wondering if I could take her. I was in decent shape, but she worked with horses for a living. I worked with patients. The patients weren't likely to put up a fight, and if they did, I'd let them go. Jaci had to work the horses, no matter if they wanted it or not. That meant her background gave her an advantage.

"I think he was in the carriage house," Jaci whispered. "I think he wanted to talk to me, to talk to Andy about what was happening. I knew Evan was afraid. I think Dave, the guy who picks up the drugs, used to pick up from Barry, I think he might have found Evan."

The knife was shaking now. I looked at her.

"We can help you. If you're the one who goes to the police, who turns yourself in..." I started.

Jaci was immediately shaking her head. She wasn't going to do that.

"I can give you the name of a good criminal lawyer. I got it when people were accusing me of having killed Marty," I said. "Go to her. She's in Frankfort, I think. Get there and turn yourself in to her and tell what you told me. If anyone can help you, she can."

The change on Jaci's face told me she was mad now. The hand stopped shaking and she glared, jaw set. "It's so easy for you. Get a lawyer. A good one. Like I can afford that."

"I can," I said. "I'll give you money. I can call her to let her know I'll pay the retainer, but that you're the client. It's the least we can do."

"I don't need your charity!" Jaci yelled. I saw her clamp her jaw as she said it, realizing she couldn't make noise, shouldn't make noise in case someone else was around there.

We all listened for someone coming. I hoped to hear the noise of someone walking down the hall. Nothing.

"I think you do," I said. "What are you going to do otherwise? Take Cheri and me hostage to get out of the state? What about the country? Can you get that far? Then what?"

Jaci was shaking her head. "Shut up."

She backed away from me, still holding the

knife. I kept my eyes on her face but tried to pick up any object that might give me a chance in my peripheral vision. The saddles on their trees would be far too difficult to try and toss at her, though I liked that they were big. The helmets were too high up on the pegs, harder to reach.

The shelves nearest me held blankets, a few baby wipes and assorted cleaners. A bin tucked into one of the shelves held extra shoes. Too bad they were too far to reach.

I needed something closer to me. The table to which Cheri was fastened had drawers. Drawers that probably had scissors or a pick. Small but sharp.

I moved towards Cheri, like I was going to help her free herself.

"Get back," Jaci stepped forward, waving the knife, trying to be menacing.

Closer now. Looking at it from there, the knife was a pretty small thing. It could still do damage if she used it against me. However, the point wasn't long enough to kill me unless she got very lucky.

I jumped forward, surprising her.

Jaci swung the knife at me.

I stepped back, reaching out at the same time.

I grabbed her arm and squeezed.

She pushed herself towards me, trying to break my hold.

I angled away from her so that the knife moved forward but not towards me. All my tai chi had paid off.

I pushed her arm down towards the table hoping to break her hold on the knife.

No such luck. I couldn't get her to drop it.

Cheri brought up her foot and kicked Jaci in the stomach.

An "ooph" sound and Jaci pulled back, trying to avoid Cheri's next kick.

I let Jaci go.

Her momentum took her backward, falling down to the floor, near the saddle trees. Her knife lay halfway between her and Cheri.

The table kept me from it.

I got to the drawer and pulled out a scissors.

Now it was my turn to hold the sharp object and look menacing.

I walked towards her shaking the scissors a bit so she could see the sharp tip. "Now, get up and we're going to the police."

Jaci gave me a long look but she didn't move.

Figuring she was just out from Cheri's kicks, I started to undo Cheri's bindings, which were tied firm and tight.

Cheri was about free when Jaci made her move. She leaped up and scurried to the door before I had a chance to let go of Cheri. I heard her running down the hall in the barn.

In that split second, I had to decide whether I would leave Cheri or hurry after Jaci. Cheri made the decision for me, pushing me away. I ran out the door and into the barn.

Chapter 34

I passed one of our boarders, pushing by him, not even recognizing him as I followed Jaci down the hall.

"What's going on?" he called after me.

A tall woman, another one of our boarders, a name forgotten in my haste, held onto her horse's bridle and frowned. Stray images of brown hair tucked up under a helmet and a blue shirt were all I glimpsed.

I wondered what she thought as first Jaci and then I went running by. I'd left the scissors with Cheri. She was free enough that she could cut through the rest of her bindings and call the police. At least I hoped so. My phone still hadn't been charged and was long dead. It hadn't been a priority earlier.

Jaci was out of the barn. The sun was low in the sky, which was pink and purple and blue off on the horizon, though it was still plenty bright outside. She crossed to the parking area.

I followed.

Then stopped.

A truck was there, and a man held a rifle, pointing it towards me. Jaci skidded to her own halt behind him.

"The police are around up at the house. They'll hear!" she yelled.

"Get in," he said. "She'll still be dead. Serve her right for interfering," the man said.

He was thin and wiry, dark haired with dark eyes. He was wearing jeans and boots with steel tips on them, good for kicking, for protecting his own feet without a care for anyone else. He was middle aged at least, a weathered face that could have been someone who spent too much time in the sun or could have been someone who smoked and drank too much. Hard to say.

Skinny threads of hair tumbled around his head, the sort that's too flyaway to do much with, and he'd just tied his back in a short pony tail that somehow made him look older and less hip rather than the other way around.

I didn't move.

"Drop it!" A voice yelled. I didn't turn, didn't dare move.

I heard footsteps on the gravel to my left and a little in front of me. I glanced that way as the rifle swung towards the voice. It wasn't Byron. It was another officer, perhaps the one who had been sent to watch Jaci. Where was Byron and why wasn't he there?

"Don't even think about it!" another voice said. This time it was Byron, and he was with yet another officer, holding guns on the man with the rifle.

"Set the rifle down slowly," Byron ordered.

The man was now facing Byron, having swung around. He let the rifle clatter to the ground, the nose pointing dangerously close to Byron. Despite the clatter and clang, the only shot towards Byron was one lone rock, dislodged from the parking area.

"You stupid bitch," the man spat at Jaci.

"No one asked you to come here. No one asked you to burn down the house," she snapped.

"You're both under arrest and will have plenty of time to tell your stories," Byron said. He and the other officer came up and started cuffing them while the third man held his gun on the two of them.

I took a step back, felt someone at my own back and whirled around. It was Cheri. She was holding the scarf that had been stuffed in her mouth, a thin thing of pale pink and yellow and beige. Behind her were several of our boarders, probably everyone who was even close to the barn.

The woman with the horse was peeking out, keeping her horse back in the barn, though she held her arm out like she was still holding the bridle.

I moved back, away from where Jaci was arguing with the other man, the one who had practically confessed.

"What's happening?" one of them asked.

Byron and the other officers—there were now four of them—didn't hear. Even if they did, I'm sure they wouldn't have answered.

I started to turn to the group and say something. Cheri put a hand on my arm.

I looked back at her and noticed Byron walking towards us.

"I'll need you to tell me what happened and what you were doing in the barn with Jaci," he said. "You were aware that she was under surveillance?"

"We were just looking around in the office," I said. "I also wanted to make sure that nothing had been taken from the tack room that shouldn't have been."

Cheri nodded. "It was my idea that if Jaci were doing something illegal that she might be trying to steal money too. I wanted Ash to be sure the books looked okay. Then we went to the tack room."

Byron looked from me to Cheri and back again. I almost saw the wheels in his head turning, trying to make sense of our comments. But there weren't really any holes in our story.

"I thought you would have found Jaci by now," I said. "Especially since her door was open upstairs. I couldn't imagine that you'd leave that open if the police hadn't been through there."

I hoped I looked innocent enough.

Finally, Byron gave a nod, though I could see he wasn't quite thrilled with my response.

"I worry about you," he said to me. "Bad enough that you get involved in these things as a suspect. I hate it when the real criminals come after you."

"I'll work on that," I said quietly, smiling.

Chapter 35

Over the next few days, it came out the way Cheri and I had put the story together. According to Jaci, Andy had killed Barry by accident when Barry had lost a shipment of drugs.

I guess Layla had gotten to the old Willard barn in time to try and save Barry and talk sense into Andy. He'd hit her, which was when she lost her earring. That gave Barry an opening to try and take down Andy. Andy had prevailed.

At least that was his story. No one alive was around to corroborate the tale.

Andy also claimed that Layla was wanting more money for her part in drug running thanks to Barry's death. He felt like she was blackmailing him. That story held up a bit better among those who knew Layla. No one really believed she'd feel terrible about someone getting killed.

Or course, speaking ill of the dead when there was such amazing gossip was part and parcel of a small town sometimes, so maybe she did have a conscience.

Andy moved her body to the strip mall, hoping that one of us would get in the crosshairs of the investigation.

As to why Evan left, no one really knew. We had Jaci's opinion that Evan was afraid of Andy, but Andy denied that. He said he didn't know why his husband had left him. Evan had been in the carriage house. Again, no one was certain why, although it was really not a place anyone would look for him.

Dave Michaels, the man who had pulled a gun on me, had been nosing around the house. He hadn't followed me—if anyone had, it was probably Evan—but later that night he'd seen shadows in the carriage house and had broken in. He'd killed Evan when he'd banged Evan's head against the edge of the granite counter.

Evan had been dead before the fire was started, which was a small mercy, and I'm sure some cold comfort to Elle.

Win had broken down and started crying. She'd known that Jaci was mixed up in drugs but wasn't sure how. She knew the names of some of the players because she often went out to the barn to pet the horses. She never talked about it, but she loved them.

Win had been embarrassed that she'd known nothing about horses or even who to ask about learning about them. She'd not even told Gram, another thing my grandmother had missed, but I decided I'd make sure our next head groom would find some time to teach Win to ride.

Daisy said she'd make sure Win had full use of Blackjax. Both of us knew he was likely to be a bit of a handful, but if we lost any boarders, I was happy to adopt a gentle, older horse for Win to learn to ride. Heck, a horse like that would be the perfect mount for me, too.

"I guess that reading items isn't all that helpful, is it?" Cheri had said to me the day after.

"Only if they're personal items," I said.

"Then here, touch this," she said, holding out a tiny golden earring stud.

"What is it?" I asked.

"Just do it," she said.

I touched it, closing my eyes, opening myself. The earring felt masculine. It had belonged to a male with an energy I wasn't familiar with. There was anxiety and hope and fear and pride and joy in the rainbow of emotions cycled through me as I started getting impressions. There was a hesitation, a nervousness about pain when the ear was pierced. I saw where it had been done at a little jeweler by the grocery store mall. The store had gone out of business before I came home from the Northwest, but apparently they'd done ear piercings.

The dark-haired girl who had done it was pretty and I felt the admiration for her smile and for other parts of her body.

That passed quickly. I saw images of other women, women that were liked, were lusted for, admired, hated. Then I saw Cheri. Her image was like a diamond. In fact that was the image I got of her, a diamond, something to be sought after and enjoyed. I saw Cheri laughing, her head tilted just so.

I got a glimpse of bedsheets and skin, and I pulled myself out of that particular vision quickly. Somethings I did not want to know.

"Travis?" I asked.

Cheri nodded. "And?"

"And what?" I asked, knowing she wanted something from me but not certain what it was other than reassurance, but about what I didn't know.

"Is he the one?" she asked.

"That I don't know," I said. "But he certainly does like you. I got an impression of a diamond, something incredibly precious and almost out of reach, something that needed to be sought after. I don't always get good impressions."

I hoped I was giving her what she wanted.

I must have because Cheri threw her arms around me and hugged me, almost giddy. I had a feeling that she and Travis were going to be very serious.

Once Dave, Jaci, and Andy were all arrested and awaiting trial, Byron had been able to start seeing me again, which was wonderful.

We'd been on three dates. We talked about his relationship with Sandra Fletcher. She'd cancelled her appointments the week after I had an official date with Byron, out at the main Seales Tavern where everyone went. No doubt word got around.

We also talked about what he wanted from life. He liked living in a rural area and wanted to continue to be a police officer there. He had no desire to leave. He also wanted a family and didn't want to wait too much longer because he wanted to be young enough to enjoy kids.

That scared me a bit, because while I want family, I'm not sure I'm ready to settle and start having babies. I had a business to build. I was also a bit afraid of telling him more about my talent.

We laughed a bit when I told him about the taking it slow on the family part.

"It seems like one of us is always about taking

it slow," Byron said, but there was laughter in that comment, an irony of what was going on.

We were in his comfortable living room, a masculine living area in a townhouse on the far side of town. It wasn't the best area, but it wasn't the worst. He had a tidy brown and cream kitchen with a decent amount of cabinet space and a tiny pantry for canned goods and such.

The kitchen flowed into the living area, the whole thing floored in a reddish brown vinyl plank. Byron had a large beige sectional sofa that took up most of the space, and it faced a big flat screen television. It was a comfortable room for movies and popcorn.

He sat with his arm around my shoulders. We were talking and eating popcorn, watching an action movie, of which he was a fan. I hadn't even suggested a romantic comedy because there seemed to be so many threads we had to work out.

But that was what taking it slow meant in a relationship.

It meant long slow kisses that ended with anticipation for more rather than grabbing what we could in that moment. It seemed like if things worked out there would be plenty of time for more. That's about all anyone can hope for, right?

Author's Note

Anyone who drives through Central Kentucky from Versailles to Frankfort will know I played fast and loose with geography in that area. There is no Seales and no Bram County. However, the town itself was inspired by Woodford County Kentucky and its environs, which residents will recognize.

All of the people are purely fictional. I have taken great liberties with the small police department in Seales and made it fit what I needed.

Ash's friends from Vancouver, Washington, Lisa and Barb, are inspired by friends from acupuncture school and acupuncture practice. Neither of them have had to keep a secret about my psychic abilities because I have none. Like Ash, I miss my friends (not just Lisa and Barb) from the Pacific Northwest, but this part of my life has taken me elsewhere and made me learn that there are many places in the U.S. that are beautiful and have their own flavor.

Enjoy your reading, and if you get a chance to drive through Kentucky, enjoy the ride through some beautiful rolling hills.

About Bonnie Elizabeth

Bonnie Elizabeth could never decide what to do, so she wrote stories about amazing things and sometimes she even finished them.

While rejection stung her so badly in person, she spent most of her young life talking to cats and dogs rather than people, she was unusually resilient when it came to rejections on her writing, racking up a good number of them.

Floating through a variety of jobs, including veterinary receptionist, cemetery administrator, and finally acupuncturist, she continued to write stories.

When the internet came along (yes she's old), she started blogging as her cat, because we all know cats don't notice rejection. Then she started publishing.

Bonnie writes in a variety of genres. Her popular Whisper series is contemporary fantasy and her Teenage Fairy Godmother series is written for teens. She has been published in a number of anthologies and is working on expanding her writing repertoire.

She lives with her husband (who talks less than she does) and her three cats, who always talk back.

Stay in Touch

Also by Bonnie Elizabeth

The Whisper Novels

Whisper Bound

Taken by the Sound

An Air of Suspicion

Little Dog Lost

Death Interrupted

Down in Whisper

A Haunting Whisper

A Haunting Attraction

Secrets Not Whispers

Only Human

Appalachian Souls Series

Souls Lost

Souls Broken

Other Novels

One Bad Wish

Sun Spot Magic

Ghosts from the Past

Unnatural Secrets

Find them all at your favorite bookseller or check us out at MyBigFatOrangeCat.com

www.ingramcontent.com/pod-product-compliance
Lightning Source LLC
Chambersburg PA
CBHW020323030826
48979CB00022B/817